Vanishing
Clues

BOOKS BY GILBERT MORRIS

TIME NAVIGATORS
(Early Teen Fiction, ages 11–14)

1. *Dangerous Voyage*
2. *Vanishing Clues*

THE HOUSE OF WINSLOW SERIES

★ ★ ★ ★

1. *The Honorable Imposter*
2. *The Captive Bride*
3. *The Indentured Heart*
4. *The Gentle Rebel*
5. *The Saintly Buccaneer*
6. *The Holy Warrior*
7. *The Reluctant Bridegroom*
8. *The Last Confederate*
9. *The Dixie Widow*
10. *The Wounded Yankee*
11. *The Union Belle*
12. *The Final Adversary*
13. *The Crossed Sabres*
14. *The Valiant Gunman*
15. *The Gallant Outlaw*
16. *The Jeweled Spur*
17. *The Yukon Queen*
18. *The Rough Rider*
19. *The Iron Lady*

THE LIBERTY BELL

1. *Sound the Trumpet*
2. *Song in a Strange Land*

CHENEY DUVALL, M.D.
(with Lynn Morris)

1. *The Stars for a Light*
2. *Shadow of the Mountains*
3. *A City Not Forsaken*
4. *Toward the Sunrising*

9605

Vanishing
Clues

Gilbert Morris

BETHANY HOUSE PUBLISHERS
MINNEAPOLIS, MINNESOTA 55438

Vanishing Clues
Copyright © 1996
Gilbert Morris

Cover illustration by Lino Saffioti.

Published by Bethany House Publishers
A Ministry of Bethany Fellowship, Inc.
11300 Hampshire Avenue South
Minneapolis, Minnesota 55438

Printed in the United States of America.

Library of Congress Cataloging-in-Publication Data

Morris, Gilbert.
    Vanishing clues / Gilbert Morris.
        p.   cm. — (The time navigators ; book 2)
    Summary: In order to earn money to help their sick younger brother and in hopes of locating their missing father, twins Danny and Dixie Fortune agree to further test their great-uncles' Chrono-Shuttle by traveling back to the time of the French and Indian War and meeting George Washington.
    [1. Time travel—Fiction. 2. Washington, George, 1732–1799—Fiction. 3. Twins—Fiction. 4. Brothers and sisters—Fiction. 5. Christian life—Fiction.] I. Title. II. Series: Morris, Gilbert. Time navigators ; 2.
PZ7.M8279Van   1996
[Fic]—dc20   96–4501
ISBN 1-55661-396-2   CIP
                                                          AC

To Dixie Lynn Morris—
Thanks for all the joy you have brought into my life!

GILBERT MORRIS spent ten years as a pastor before becoming Professor of English at Ouachita Baptist University in Arkansas and earning a Ph.D. at the University of Arkansas. During the summers of 1984 and 1985 he did postgraduate work at the University of London. A prolific writer, he has had over 25 scholarly articles and 200 poems published in various periodicals, and over the past years has had more than 70 novels published. His family includes three grown children, and he and his wife live in Orange Beach, Alabama.

1

Some days, everything goes wrong. But why does today have to be one of those days? Fourteen-year-old Danny Fortune stumbled in his mad rush to find a clean pair of jeans. His alarm had failed to go off, and the school bus would be arriving in five minutes. It definitely felt like Monday.

"Danny, you ready yet?" his twin sister, Dixie, called through the door. "You're not going to have time to grab any breakfast."

Thanks for the reminder, Danny thought, but he put a clamp on the response—Dixie wasn't trying to annoy him. "Coming!" he shouted as he stooped to duck his wavy hair under the faucet. The curls were going in ten different directions at once.

When Danny and his sister boarded the bus a few minutes later, he was out of breath. *The rest of the day has to go better*, he told himself.

It didn't, thanks to P.E. Danny's basketball team was playing one made up of players from another grade, and a crowd of students had gathered to watch. It was the final game of a tournament between classes, and those who were in study hall were excused to cheer on their team.

Normally, Danny wasn't a stand-out on the basketball court, but today he had a feeling that he was going to shine. At least, he wanted to do well—the girl of his dreams, Courtney Johnson, was in the stands watching.

With long, blond hair, a fabulous smile, and striking blue eyes, Courtney was hard not to like. All semester, Danny had been trying to work up the courage to ask her out. The only catch was, Courtney had never even breathed a word to him—she was fifteen, after all, and not interested in dating anyone a year younger. Despite the difference in their ages, Danny got to see quite a bit of Courtney, who wasn't exactly the brightest girl in the world. She was repeating several classes, and Danny was fortunate enough to be in all of them.

All through the first half of the game—and for most of the second—Danny did time as a bench warmer. He kept hoping Coach Jeffers would call out, "Fortune! Get in there to save the game!"

But it didn't happen. Danny slumped back resignedly, his head down, waiting for the game to end.

Suddenly, a needle-sharp elbow jabbed his rib.

"Hey, Danny! Coach is telling you to go in."

Danny looked up—sure enough, Coach Jeffers was waving at him, a frown fixed on his face.

"Fortune," he snapped, "we've got to give Ted here a break. You fill in—and *try* not to do too much damage. Got it?"

"Sure, Coach!" Danny responded eagerly. He ran out onto the court, praying for that magic moment when he would save the game and an adoring Courtney would throw her arms around him, crying, "My hero!"

But as the game dragged on, it became clear that none of his teammates had the least interest in Danny saving the game. In fact, no one would even pass him the ball.

"Hey, this isn't a four-man team, you know. Throw me the ball," Danny shouted between huffs.

"Right. You'd probably lose it," Ed Coulter shot back. "And we can't afford to let them score another point."

Finally, with only two minutes to play, Danny seized the ball at half court. The other team's net swayed invitingly. *I can make this*, he thought as he headed down court.

A few steps into his run, he decided to try out a fancy dribble he had been practicing in the hope that Courtney would appreciate his innovative moves. Veering to the right, he glanced up—Courtney was on her feet, baby blues fixed on him.

At last! he thought. *She sees me!*

In the next instant, the ball disappeared.

Danny wheeled around as Ed shouted, "Watch out, Fortune!"

But it was too late. One of the opposing players had snatched the ball, and Danny didn't have a chance of catching him. The guy stopped, aiming a perfect shot. The buzzer went off as the ball swished through the net, sending Danny's hopes plummeting with it to the floor.

Deflated, Danny glanced up into the bleachers to see Courtney and her friends giggling and pointing down at him. It was too much to take. He turned and left the gym so angry with himself it hardly registered when someone said, "Ease up, Dan. It's only a game."

Danny managed to shower and dress without saying a word to anyone. *As if anyone wants to be seen talking to me after that lousy play.* As he left the gym to head for his last class, he frowned. *At least I've had all the bad breaks I possibly can squeeze into one day.*

But he was wrong. Danny managed to run into trouble within ten minutes of walking into Mrs. Simpkins' American history class.

Mrs. Simpkins, a tall woman who looked as if she might snap in a strong wind, took obvious pride in her knowledge of American history. Unfortunately, her version of history was usually based more on opinion than fact.

Danny slipped into his seat at the back of the class, hoping none of his classmates had witnessed the disaster in the gym. A warm hand touched his shoulder, and he turned to look up at Dixie.

"Don't worry about it, Danny," she said. "There's more to life than basketball."

What does it matter, Danny argued inwardly, *when I still have to make it through today!*

Frustrated, he decided to do his best not to mess up again—but Mrs. Simpkins, who was already engrossed in her lecture on the famous *Mayflower* voyage, wasn't in on the decision.

"To make a difficult situation worse," she droned, "the people aboard the *Mayflower* had to suffer through a long trip without any hot food."

Before he could think the better of it, Danny spoke up. "But that isn't true! The Pilgrims were able to cook on the *Mayflower*—at least once in a while."

The whole class swiveled to look at Danny—including Courtney, who was repeating the class for the third time.

Danny felt his face grow hot, but he held his ground. "The ship had a galley, and every third day the crew let the passengers use it. They made a charcoal fire over some sand on an iron hearth, where they were able to cook porridge made from soaked oats. They ate it cold the other days."

Mrs. Simpkins glared at him. "Oh?" she asked sarcastically. "And just where did you find that information, Mr. Danny Fortune?"

Danny wanted to say, "From my trip on the *Mayflower*, of course!" but he knew that would sound ridiculous and land him in detention—never mind that it was true.

"I . . . I don't exactly remember the source, but I'm sure that's what it said." The half truth made him cringe inside.

"Well, *I* would like to have the reference to that particular bit of historical information, Mr. Fortune," Mrs. Simpkins stated grimly.

Danny mumbled an apology, his face flaming. "I wish I could give it, Mrs. Simpkins. I just wasn't thinking."

"*That* is apparent." Mrs. Simpkins harrumphed and resumed dispensing misinformation about the *Mayflower*.

As the class ended and Danny stood to walk out, he heard a soft voice whisper, "Danny?"

He turned—it was Courtney!

"Don't pay any attention to Mrs. Simpkins," Courtney said with a smile. "I was glad you stood up to her."

Knowing she was so close made Danny's mouth stop working. He mumbled something incoherent, then she was gone.

Great, he thought bitterly. *Now she really thinks I'm an idiot!*

On their way home, Dixie said, "I was afraid you were going to blurt out our whole story in history, Danny."

"I nearly did," Danny confessed. "I was so mad, I nearly told that old beanpole what it really was like living on the *Mayflower*."

"Don't ever do that!" Dixie exclaimed, grabbing Danny by the arm and forcing him to look into her eyes. "If we told anyone we'd actually gone back in time, they'd have us locked up! I mean, would *you* believe us?"

Danny grew quiet, remembering their time-travel trip to the 1620s—the *Mayflower* voyage and that long, hard first year of life in the New World. The twins' great-uncles, Mordecai and Zacharias Fortune—one an historian, and the other an inventor—had sent the two into the past when they had come to them seeking financial help following the mysterious disappearance of their father, James. The twins had gotten the money they needed—ten thousand dollars. All they had to do in exchange was undertake a risky voyage back in time!

Fortunately, their great-uncles' scheme had worked. The twins had returned safely to the present—and even more surprisingly, on the same date they had left. The whole trip had taken no more than a few hours.

"You know," Danny began, "I still can't believe Mordecai and Zacharias tried to keep Dad's whereabouts secret from us. They knew he'd used the Chrono-Shuttle to slip into the past, but they wouldn't tell us the truth until they were sure we wouldn't do any more time traveling for them otherwise."

Dixie nodded. "From the moment I met them, I knew those two were up to something. But the important thing now is that we need their help—if you can call it that—to find Dad."

They reached their apartment and found their five-year-old brother, Jimmy, alone in the middle of a pile of books.

"Hi!" he said brightly. "My sitter went home early."

Danny couldn't believe what he was hearing—Jimmy had cystic fibrosis and it wasn't safe to leave him unattended. "She shouldn't have done that! Anything could have happened!"

"It's okay," Jimmy reassured him. "Dixie, want to play Go Fish with me?"

"Not now, I've got to make us an early supper. You can play with Danny until Mom gets home."

"Danny, if you want, you can read to me instead."

Danny picked up the worn Bible storybook that was his brother's favorite. "Take your pick, buddy."

"How about the one where David knocks off Goliath?" Jimmy suggested.

"You know it by heart, but I'll read it anyway," Danny laughed. While he was reading, the front door opened and their mother walked in and quickly eased out of her new trench coat.

"Hi, Mom," Danny said cheerfully. "You're home early."

At five feet ten, Ellen Fortune was taller than average, and her fine blond hair, dark blue eyes, and pretty features made her look much younger than her thirty-six years. She came across the room and bent over to kiss Jimmy, then gave Danny a hug. "How are my boys?" she asked.

Something in her voice caused Danny to give her a second look.

"We're all fine," he replied. "How are you?"

"Oh, all right." Ellen moved quickly toward the bathroom. "I'm just going to wash up before supper."

"I'd better go help Dixie set the table, Jimmy." Danny patted his little brother on the back. "You can finish the story yourself. You know it as well as I do."

He went into the kitchen and leaned in toward his sister, who was chopping carrots. "Dix, don't get upset, but I think something's wrong. Mom looks worried."

Dixie frowned. "Do you suppose she's going to change her mind about letting us visit our great-uncles tonight?"

"I don't know. I hope not."

They set the table, put the food on, and everyone sat down. Jimmy said the blessing, stretching out his thank-you's for a full three minutes.

Danny and Dixie exchanged a glance. *He's the one who's sick*, Danny thought, *yet he's the most thankful person here.*

All through the meal, they managed to keep a conversation going, but Danny noticed their mother said almost nothing. *What could possibly be wrong?* he wondered.

The twins finally had a chance to ask her after supper while they washed dishes. Jimmy was in the living room watching TV.

"Did you have a hard day, Mom?" Dixie prodded.

"Well, not at work," Ellen replied hesitantly. "I stopped by the clinic on the way home."

Something about her tone of voice gave Danny a bad feeling. "Are Jimmy's test results back?"

Their mother nodded. "Yes, they are—and they aren't very good."

Dixie licked her lips, then asked, "What happens next?"

"His specialist says Jimmy should try a new treatment, but it's very expensive. Several thousand dollars. I know we still have some money left from your father's uncles, but I don't know how long it will last if we have to . . . if this treatment doesn't work—" Ellen broke off, and Danny spotted the glint of tears in her eyes.

"Don't cry, Mom," he said softly. "We'll find a way."

"How?" Ellen asked hopelessly. "I can't possibly impose on Mordecai and Zacharias for more money."

Dixie said quickly, "God will take care of us, Mom. You'll see!"

Ellen gave them a wan smile. "I honestly don't know what I'd do without you two. I wish I had your faith. If only your father . . ." She glanced down at her watch. "Oh, look at the time! You two are going to have to catch a cab right away if you're still going to help out Zacharias and Mordecai tonight. We can't let them down—not after everything they've done to help."

Some help they've been, Danny thought. *If Dad had never gone to see them, he wouldn't be missing, and we'd be in much better shape right now!*

Dixie moved to grab her jean jacket. "You're right, Mom. We shouldn't keep our great-uncles waiting, and we have a big day ahead tomorrow in school."

As the twins left the apartment to wait for their cab, Danny turned to Dixie, who was fidgeting nervously with her backpack. "I know you don't want to do this, sis, but it's too late to say no. As dangerous as it may be, we've got to go back in time at least one more time—for Jimmy, for Mom—and for Dad."

2

"You want me to wait?" the cab driver asked. The dried-up little man reached with a trembling hand for his can of soda. Glancing toward the hulking gray house set deep into a grove of pines, he gulped and said, "Don't bring many people out to this place. You sure this is the right address?"

Danny pulled the fare out of his pocket and handed it to the man. "Yes, this is it. We'll give you a call when we're ready to go—shouldn't be too late."

The driver snorted, barely hesitating long enough for the twins to exit before roaring off in a cloud of dust. An eerie silence settled on the pair.

"He's afraid of this place," Dixie whispered, looking around as if she agreed with the cabby. The dilapidated old house with its heavily draped windows was anything but inviting, particularly in the evening. A little shiver passed through her. "I don't like it much myself," she admitted. "Reminds me of *Addams Family* reruns."

Danny felt the same way but thought he had to show more courage. "It's just an old house," he shrugged. "It isn't nearly as spooky inside. Let's get this over with."

Danny and Dixie walked up to the massive door, and Danny pulled the rope that dangled from the ceiling of

17

the porch. "You'd think an inventor like Zacharias could do better than this for a doorbell," he muttered.

The door opened with a creaking noise, and a threatening figure filled the doorway. "What do you want?" it rumbled.

Danny said, "It's just us, Toombs. We've come to see our great-uncles."

The gigantic butler glared down at them from his full height, his tiny eyes gleaming. "Oh, it's you," he grunted. "They're expecting you."

The twins stepped inside and followed Toombs up the huge winding staircase to a large wood door. The giant rapped on it, and an irritated voice answered, "Are they here yet?"

Toombs swung the door wide and stepped back, allowing Danny and Dixie to enter.

As usual, Mordecai Fortune was half buried in the mound of books and papers that cluttered his desk. A short, thin man with white hair, sharp black eyes, and a dark complexion, he wore a faded old suit—so shapeless it hung on his body as if it had been bought for a much larger man.

"Come in and sit down!" he insisted as he got up from his chair. "Zacharias! Come quickly!" he called out, then turned to the twins. "We've been waiting for you. What's taken so long?"

Before either of them could answer, another man entered through a narrow side door. An exact replica of Mordecai except for his white lab coat, this was Zacharias, the inventor of the Chrono-Shuttle that made time travel possible. He hurried over and said abruptly,

"About time you got here! We were nearly ready to hire someone else to test the Chrono-Shuttle."

"Right," Danny snorted. "You won't find many volunteers willing to put their life on the line and keep quiet about it."

With a sharp glance at her brother, Dixie interrupted. "We're sorry to be late, sir. But we're here now."

"And not a moment too soon!" Mordecai snapped.

Danny swallowed hard and forced himself to remain friendly—it wouldn't do to upset their great-uncles so much that he ruined their only hope of finding their father. "There's one other thing. I know we're going to search for our dad, but since you lost him, it's only fair that you pay us"—at the angry gleam in Zacharias's eye, Danny rushed to finish—"not as much as last time, but maybe a couple of thousand dollars. Our little brother needs a new treatment, and it's going to cost a lot."

Zacharias shook his head. "We've already given you ten thousand dollars. We're not made of money, you know!"

Mordecai raised a hand as if to calm his brother. "We'll do the best we can. But as my brother says, there *is* a limit to our finances. Inventing is an expensive line of work."

Danny nodded gratefully. He suspected that, despite their protests and rundown home, their great-uncles had plenty of money. "We'll need payment in advance again, please. Cash."

Mordecai made a show of noisily removing the money from a corner safe, counting it out, and handing it to Danny. "There!" he said grumpily. "You'd think family would at least trust one another!"

"It'd be easier if *family* had taken better care of our father." Danny didn't want to argue with these men, but he was still upset that they had used his father as a guinea pig in their dangerous experiments.

"Before we go any further, let's talk for one minute about that Recall Unit," Dixie said. "Are you sure it will work again?"

The question seemed to irritate Zacharias. "Of course it will work!" the little man sputtered. "I'm a scientist—one of the greatest inventors who ever lived, if I do say so myself. When I do something, I do it right!"

"Well, you've obviously made some mistakes," Danny retorted, "or our father would be at home right now!"

Dixie intervened. "But let's not argue about Dad's faulty Recall Unit. It's too late now. Let's get down to business. Uncle Mordecai," she nodded in his direction, "has told us that our best bet of finding Dad is to return to the time of the French and Indian War."

Mordecai nodded briefly. "Yes. Your father had the makings of a fine historian—like me," he added. "I was doing so well with him. It was unfortunate that he chose to rig the Chrono-Shuttle and slip into the past on his own."

"I warned him never to use the machine unless I was there!" Zacharias pointed out. "But he's like all Fortunes"—here he gave Danny a hard look—"stubborn. Nearly impossible to work with!"

Mordecai nodded. "As true as that is, dear brother, I do feel some responsibility, however undeserved, for James's disappearance. The Recall Unit he took *wasn't* powerful enough to transport him home, and I'm afraid some of our . . . chats . . . about history made him overly anxious to prove some of his crazy theories."

"What kind of theories?" Dixie asked.

"Oh . . . he had this ridiculous notion that people really were as decent and fine and honorable as they are in the history books." Mordecai's eyes sparked. "Everyone knows that most of the so-called heroes we read about weren't heroes at all. Historians tend to ignore people's faults and make up stories and legends about them that have no basis in fact. As you know, one of the reasons I asked Zacharias to invent the Chrono-Shuttle was to prove that our history books are full of nothing but lies."

Dixie laughed. "Well, you didn't exactly prove your point when we traveled back to the time of the *Mayflower* and the Pilgrims. The Saints turned out to be good and honest Christian people, didn't they, Danny?"

Danny grinned and nodded.

Mordecai discounted Dixie's comment. "We've only conducted *one* experiment. No responsible scientist builds a theory on one set of test results. This time, we're going to learn the truth about a man the entire country—no, the whole world—has idolized."

"George Washington?" Danny guessed.

"Exactly!" Mordecai bobbed his head vigorously before continuing. "The 'father' of this country! The boy who couldn't tell a lie! The man who in the beginning held this whole nation together!" He shook his head fiercely. "At least, that's what all the history books say— but I don't believe a word of it. George Washington was undoubtedly an opportunist—no better than our modern politicians! It's up to you two to prove my point," he added angrily.

Zacharias broke in, "Your father talked a lot about Washington, especially the last night he was here. Studying the man was one of his pet projects. In fact, the last argument we had, he insisted he would prove us wrong."

"That's right," Mordecai said. " 'I'll show you George Washington was as fine a man as the history books say!' he said." The little man stopped, shrugged, and went on, "And that same night, he disappeared."

Zacharias nodded. "We think he traveled back into time to meet George Washington."

"Wouldn't he have gone back to the time of the American Revolution?" Dixie asked.

Mordecai stroked his chin as if considering the idea, then shook his head. "No," he replied slowly, "I still think he's gone back to 1755 and the French and Indian War, or close to that year."

"He did talk a lot about Washington's younger years," Zacharias agreed. "An awful lot."

Mordecai nodded. "That last night, only hours before he disappeared, he read me some passages about young Washington's leadership during the French and Indian War. He said, 'I'll prove to you that Washington was a good man even when he was young.' For that reason, I think he's traveled back to the year 1755—the year Washington was with General Braddock in the attack on Fort Duquesne."

Zacharias was growing impatient. "Well, what are

you two waiting for?" he demanded.

Danny shrugged. "I'm as ready as I'll ever be, I guess."

"The sooner we find our father, the sooner we can end these dangerous experiments," Dixie said. "I'm ready, too."

"I think we've got a good chance of locating him this time," Mordecai put in, an excited gleam in his piercing black eyes. "Now, let's prepare you for this trip."

During the next hour, the twins were briefed on what to expect in terms of speech and customs, and dressed for the time period.

Dixie slipped into a simple gray cotton dress that reached her ankles.

"Why can't I tell the right shoe from the left?" she asked when she went to put on the heavy shoes.

Mordecai chuckled. "Because there isn't a difference. No one made a distinction between left and right feet in the 1750s."

Danny had on a pair of brown trousers, a pair of short brown boots, a gray shirt, and a short jacket to go over it.

"It may be a little chilly when you get there," Mordecai warned. "So take some money to buy heavier clothing if necessary."

Danny inspected the gold coins his great-uncle handed him and asked, "Are these the real thing?"

"Of course they're real!" Mordecai snapped. "You think I'd get you arrested for counterfeiting? Now, remember what I told you, and you'll be fine. Be careful not to let anyone know who you really are or interfere in historical events. We can't go changing history!"

"That should do it, then." Zacharias rubbed his hands together. "Let's head to the laboratory so we can send you on your way." He led the twins out of the office down to his basement laboratory.

Danny felt a prickle of fear as he recalled their last experience in this laboratory—just a few short days ago. *Remember, you're doing this for Dad*, he told himself.

Fluorescent lights lined the ceiling of the massive room, casting an otherworldly gleam on the dozens of odd contraptions crammed into the space. Wires and glass tubes ran everywhere. In the center of the room was Zacharias's crowning achievement: the Chrono-Shuttle.

Dixie whispered to Danny, "I don't know why, but just looking at that thing makes me nervous!"

A large, glass-domed machine with an eerie green glow, the Chrono-Shuttle was like something out of a science-fiction movie. The glass exterior gave Danny a clear view of the two chairs and monitor inside. Countless wires ran through the glass tubing wrapped around the rear of the contraption.

Zacharias approached the large console that controlled the Chrono-Shuttle. "Remember these two buttons? They control your location by setting latitude and longitude. In other words, you can pinpoint any spot on earth, adjust the settings, and—*boom!*—you're there." He laughed as the twins started at the *boom*. "I've already determined your location. You'll materialize near a small fort—the location will give you a good feel for life at that time."

Then he gestured toward the panel's digital clock. "This, as you will remember, sets the destination time."

Danny said, "The controls look easy enough to operate—I just wish I understood how the Chrono-Shuttle works."

"It's not your job to understand it," Zacharias said impatiently. "All you need to do is travel in it."

"Let's get this over with, Danny," Dixie suggested. Her pale face told her brother she was growing nervous.

Zacharias opened the door of the domed machine, and they climbed carefully inside.

"Ready," Danny announced.

"Not quite." Zacharias leaned forward and handed them the Recall Unit, a small, thin disk that resembled an old-fashioned pocket watch. "You'll want this. Be sure you don't lose it this time. And be absolutely certain you're standing together when you push the home button. The moment you hit it, you'll be right back in the Chrono-Shuttle—unless you're standing outside of its range. Mordecai and I don't want anyone else marooned in time!"

Danny slipped the leather cord holding the Recall Unit cord over his head. The metal disk felt like ice against his chest, and he began to feel slightly anxious. As thrilling and adventurous as time travel sounded, now that he'd done it once, he wasn't eager to do it again—at least not so soon.

He glanced at his sister, who took his hand. "I sure hope we find Dad," she murmured, then covered her eyes with the other hand.

Zacharias fastened the door, and the odd green shimmer intensified, bathing them in a ring of bright light. Then Zacharias pulled the lever on the control panel, and the surge of energy caused the Chrono-Shuttle to pulsate rapidly.

As the lab and Zacharias seemed to dissolve before them, Dixie squeezed Danny's hand—so hard it hurt. Dizzy, Danny shut his eyes, and a shrill humming increased until it hurt his ears. In the next instant, it was as if the chair had dropped out from under him, and he was falling—falling as though he would never stop.

"Don't be afraid, Dixie," he tried to shout above the humming. "We'll be all right. And this time, we'll find Dad!"

3

The shrill hum of the Chrono-Shuttle faded, followed by a deep silence. Danny became aware that he was still holding Dixie's hand, but to his shock, he could not see a thing.

"Dixie!" he shouted. "I think I've gone blind!"

A voice came—his sister's. "No, Danny, you're okay. I thought the same thing for a moment. It's just the middle of the night."

Danny glanced up. Sure enough—through a thick canopy of trees, a few faint stars gleamed. He rose to his feet and wiped the sweat from his forehead. "Wow, what a scare!"

He peered into the dense blackness that surrounded them, but it was no use. The light from the few stars glittering overhead was almost blotted out by the trees that towered around them.

"Well, this is just great," he observed, frustrated. "How are we going to find anything in the middle of the night?"

Dixie moved closer to him and took his hand. "Maybe it won't be too long before it's light. Let's just sit beside a tree until then."

Danny felt silly holding his sister's hand, but he was

afraid to let go and lose her in the dark.

Together, they groped their way through the midnight darkness to the base of a huge tree and sat down.

"Maybe we should use the Recall Unit and return home. We could start over and come back at a better time," he suggested.

"No, let's just wait. Dawn can't be too far away."

The two of them waited for what seemed like hours. Just when they were reconsidering using the Recall Unit, Dixie shouted, "Look, Danny! Along the horizon."

"What is it?" Danny turned to see a sliver of light rising in the trees. "I see it!"

The twins got to their feet and kept their eyes trained on the thin white line that began to show in the east. Soon it was light enough that they could make out their surroundings, but that was not much help. They were in the middle of a forest of huge trees, larger than any they had ever seen. The trees were so thick and the branches so interlaced that there were few weeds beneath them.

"Let's get out of here and look for a stream or a spring," Danny said. "I'm really thirsty."

They moved under the branches, dodging around the huge trees, never straying very far from each other. Finally they came out into a small clearing. They walked along, looking for some sign of human habitation, but saw nothing but trees and sky.

At last Dixie said, "Isn't that a spring?"

They ran across the forest floor. Sure enough, flowing out of a big rock was a tiny spring.

Leaning over, Danny tasted it. It was so icy it hurt his teeth. "Try some, Dix. This water is incredible!"

She took a tentative sip. "You're right. You could bottle this. . . ."

A sound over to the left drew Danny's attention. He swiveled his head to see a huge form emerging from the shade of the forest—so big it made Toombs look small. His heart skipped a beat. "Dixie!" he croaked.

She looked to where he was pointing. "A bear!" she shrieked.

At the sound of her voice, the grizzly broke into a run faster than either of them would have dreamed possible. Danny grabbed his sister's arm and looked wildly around for a tree to climb, but the nearest branches were too far from the ground.

The bear lunged toward them, so close now that Danny could see its beady red eyes and long, sharp teeth. He didn't know whether to run toward the woods or across the field. Either way, it was hopeless.

"Run to those trees!" he shouted to Dixie. "He can't catch both of us!" He shoved Dixie, but she refused to go.

"No—not without you!"

The bear was now only about forty feet away, and they could hear the pounding of his massive paws on the hard-packed earth.

God, please help us! Danny cried silently.

Then, when the bear was only a few yards away, a sudden shot rang out. The angry beast collapsed, the force of its run rolling it over and over. It grunted, tried to get up, then opened its mouth and fell over.

Danny stared at the bear, his throat too dry to swallow. "Thank you, God!" he managed to whisper.

"Who killed the bear?" Dixie asked in a trembling voice.

Danny turned and spotted a muscular, tall man—so tall, he would have had to duck his head to go through most doorways—coming up over a rise with a long rifle in hand.

"Well now, young'uns," the stranger said, eyeing the twins and rubbing his stubbled chin. "That was a close one, wasn't it now?"

Danny shook his head in amazement. "He'd have gotten us for sure if you hadn't shot him. I don't know how to thank you."

The man smiled and offered a rough, weathered hand in a handshake. "Name's Joe Latimer. Shore am glad I was around to be of some help. Better load up quick in case some unfriendly ears heard that shot."

The twins introduced themselves and watched as he reloaded his gun, tilting a powder horn carefully so the powder fell into the barrel. He wrapped a ball in a piece of leather, then rammed it down the rifle barrel with the ramrod mounted underneath.

"How'd you younkers come to be out in the middle of the woods?" Latimer inquired.

Danny hesitated, trying to think of a way to give this stranger an answer he would believe without lying. "Well . . . we've gotten separated from our father, and we're trying to find him."

"If you're lost, you'd better go home with me. It ain't safe to be about in these woods alone. But first," he nodded at the dead animal, "I gotta skin that bear."

"We'll wait for you," Danny said.

They both watched as the man pulled out a huge knife, bled the bear, and began to quickly skin it. Danny had never seen anything skinned before, and he was fascinated by the way the man took the black fur off just as he might remove an overcoat. By the grimace on Dixie's face, Danny was sure his sister didn't share his admiration.

When the man began to trim some of the fat, Danny ventured, "How are you going to carry the bear home?"

"Not takin' it all home," Latimer grunted. He put some meat and fat in the hide and picked it up. "We better be gettin' on. Don't like to hang around after I've fired a shot. 'Sides, my son's waitin' on me." He turned and began walking through the thick woods.

Danny and Dixie followed. The man never looked back—except once when they fell behind. "Better hurry up," he warned. "Don't like the looks of this."

Dixie caught Danny's questioning glance. "Indians," she whispered. "I'm sure he's worried about Indians. English settlers are having a lot of trouble with them at this time. I sure wish we were somewhere else!"

"Me too!" Danny agreed.

They hurried to catch up with Latimer, who was moving faster than ever. "Had an accident in camp," he explained. "My boy got hurt—cut in the leg with an ax. It's turning bad." His dark eyes looked worried. "I hated to leave him, but I had to get something to put on that wound. 'Course, that's why I was out tracking bear."

Danny was confused. "What do bears have to do with a leg wound?"

Joe Latimer appeared surprised. Without pausing in

his rapid pace, he shot Danny a critical look. "Why, everybody knows bear fat's the thing to put on a wound to draw out the poison."

"Oh," Danny responded. *People sure did do some strange things in the old days.*

Latimer increased his pace, driving across the floor of the forest. The twins rushed to keep up, trying to imitate the quick, careful way the man walked—picking the best places to step, hardly slowing as he made his choices. It seemed Latimer knew instinctively which stones would roll, which branches would give and crackle, which underbrush should be avoided. Danny and Dixie stumbled behind as best they could.

Finally, when they were both out of breath, Latimer stopped and pointed ahead. "There's the camp. Come on now."

The small grove was almost hidden from view.

"It's me, Caleb," Latimer called out. "You awake?"

"Yes, Pa."

Latimer approached a boy who was on a makeshift bed beside a small spring. "I got the bear meat, son. You'll be all right now." Then he seemed to remember himself. "Oh. We got company, too—Danny and Dixie Fortune. I found them lost in the woods."

The twins came closer. The boy didn't look any older than fifteen. His face was red with fever, and a rough bandage made of a torn shirt was wrapped around his swollen leg.

"I'm sorry you got hurt," Dixie said.

The boy looked at her and blinked his eyes, as if he

was surprised to see her there. "Well," he muttered, "shouldn't have done that."

Danny felt like he was in the way as Latimer began to strip off the rough bandage and, without saying a word, took his knife and opened the raw wound in the boy's leg. The boy cried out, choked, then turned his face away from them and grabbed the ground, dirty finger-nails digging in.

Dixie abruptly walked away, her hand to her mouth. Danny swallowed hard.

Latimer took some bear fat and applied it to the wound before dressing it again. His face grew hard as he tried to hide his obvious concern. "Guess that's the best I can do," he said. "Bear fat's always been good for drawing poison out of a wound."

Danny tried to think of something to say. *How can this man believe that bear fat will help anything? I only hope it doesn't make the infection worse!*

"I got to get him home so his ma can tend to that leg. That's all there is to it!"

It was no surprise to Danny that Joe Latimer looked weary and worn. They had waited all day and night for his son to get better, but instead he seemed to worsen.

Danny knew that Latimer had another worry besides Caleb—Indians. They had Danny worried, too. He was growing so nervous he had started hearing things—a snap in the woods, the mysterious call of a wild animal

. . . or had it been an Indian imitating a wild animal? Danny shivered.

"Could the owl we heard last night have been an Indian?" he asked.

Latimer shrugged. "Wouldn't be surprised—they like to use owl calls. One thing's shore, it ain't safe to stay on here." He shifted and glanced quickly at his son, looking as though something disturbed him. "I guess I'll have to tote him out, but it's a long way—I don't know as I can make it."

He eyed the twins for a moment. "I could leave him here with you and go get help. Get a horse. But I hate to do that."

"No, don't do that," Danny said quickly. The thought of staying in the woods alone, especially with the wounded boy, seemed worse than anything he could think of.

"Mr. Latimer," he suggested. "Why don't we make a stretcher? We could use that bear hide you brought. You could take the front of it, and Dixie and I could take one handle apiece at the back."

Latimer blinked. "Why, Danny—I think that'll answer." He jumped up, his expression relieved. "I'll get that stretcher made right away! We got to get outta this place."

In less than an hour, the little group was on their way. Latimer had made the poles for the stretcher out of two saplings, whittling them smooth with his big knife. Then he tied most of the bear hide and one of his shirts onto the poles.

Latimer set a slow but steady pace—Danny thought

he probably wanted to avoid wearing out his help. They stopped twice before noon, pausing the second time to cook a little of the bear meat they had brought, then pushed on. By nightfall, Danny and Dixie were exhausted, their hands raw from the wood handles of the stretcher.

They built a fire and prepared to spend the night in a small clearing. "Don't reckon you young'uns can make it to our place."

"Sure we can, sir," Dixie said instantly. "We can do it. Can we get there tomorrow?"

"Yeah . . . if you're up to it, I think we can make it by noon." Latimer looked over at Caleb and asked, "How you doin', son?"

Caleb's face was still flushed with fever, but he whispered, "I'll make it, Pa. Just keep a-goin'."

Dixie got up, wet a cloth in the stream beside the camp, and came over and put it on Caleb's forehead. "I think your fever's gone down a little," she said quietly.

Caleb looked at her almost bashfully. "Thank you, Dixie." In spite of the seriousness of the situation, Danny had to grin.

The next morning they set out at dawn. After a hard morning's walk, Latimer announced, "There she is! Right over that yonder hill."

"Good," Dixie breathed as they trudged up yet another hill. "I don't think I could have gone much farther!"

Latimer led them along a well-beaten path over a rise. "There. There's my place." He pointed straight ahead.

Danny and Dixie staggered the last few yards and looked down into a little valley. Exept for a crude shack and a lean-to, the valley seemed empty. *That's it?* Danny thought in surprise. *How can a family possibly live in a place like this?*

Latimer appeared to sense their disappointment. "Indians burnt the cabin down last winter." He shrugged. "I was called to go with the militia, and the family had to stay in the fort. While we was gone, them Indians burnt it to the ground. They left the barn, though."

As he spoke, a tall, big-boned woman came out of the shack and walked rapidly toward them. She was not pretty, but her face was strong and kind. "Hello, Joe," she said. "What's happened?"

"Hello, Ruth. 'Fraid Caleb got a bad cut. We had a hard time gettin' here." He motioned toward the twins. "This here's Danny and Dixie Fortune. I come on them in the woods. If they hadn't been around, I don't know if I could've gotten Caleb home."

By now the concerned woman was leaning over her son, but she took time for one quick smile at the twins. "We thank you."

Things happened very quickly after that. A blond girl, maybe thirteen years old, came out of the shack. "This here's my daughter, Leah." Joe introduced them quickly as they settled Caleb in the shelter of the lean-to.

By the time they had finished and told their stories to Ruth and Leah, dark was coming on. "I'll fix us something to eat," Leah offered.

Night fell quickly—too quickly, Danny thought. They were sitting under the lean-to, eating one of the most unusual meals the twins had ever had.

"What is this?" Dixie asked, poking at a dark purple sausage. "I don't think I've ever had it."

"Why, just some blood sausage," Ruth answered. "That and the pig greens, sauerkraut, and smoked trout are our usual fare. You mean to say you've never eaten blood sausage?"

Danny and Dixie shook their heads, and Danny thought how he wasn't sure he wanted to even *start* eating blood sausage. It certainly wasn't something his mom would bring home from the local supermarket.

"Ruth, this lean-to ain't fit for livin' in much longer," Latimer said as he wiped the last bit of food from his plate. "We've got to build a new cabin." He lit his pipe, then, lowering his voice so his son wouldn't hear him, he observed, "Be harder now, what with Caleb laid up. Depended on him to help me cut them logs."

"We'll do what has to be done," Ruth responded calmly. "Caleb will heal." She turned to the twins. "Now, you young'uns need a place to sleep. We ain't got much, but I tell you what. We'll keep Caleb in here with us. Leah'll take you two to the barn and see that you get a place and some clean straw to sleep on. And, Leah, take a blanket for Danny. Dixie can share with you."

"Yes, Ma."

Danny was so tired he could barely move—and when

he did move, he was so sore he was sorry he had tried.

As they wrapped up in their stiff wool blanket, Dixie asked Leah, "Are the Indians really so bad?"

"'Course!" Leah said. "Least right now. You're lucky they didn't get you. They kilt one of the Ferguson boys last month, not five miles from here."

Danny didn't like the sound of that, and he was sure his sister didn't either.

"What if they come when we're asleep?" Dixie asked.

"Then we'll die," Leah said simply.

Great, thought Danny. *What have we gotten ourselves into now?*

4

"Danny!" Someone was calling his name from far off.

Danny clawed at the air around him. He seemed to be at the bottom of a deep, black pit. *How'd I get here? Have the Indians captured me? Am I dead?*

"Danny, get up right this minute!" Dixie's frustrated voice commanded.

Danny was immediately conscious of a sharp ache in his hands and back. "Ow!" he said, attempting to clench his fist. Prying his tired eyes open, he inspected his palms. Huge blisters had swollen and burst in the night. *Welcome to the eighteenth century*, he thought morosely.

"Danny, come on!"

He looked at his sister, who was already up and ready to go.

"Time for breakfast," she said. "Let's go."

He groaned as he got up from the straw, his body protesting every movement. "Dixie, look at my hands. I can hardly close them!" he complained.

Dixie showed him her own bloody hands. "Mine are just as bad. And my back feels like it's been run over!" She tried to shake her head and winced. "That was some job getting Caleb back here, wasn't it?"

Danny left the barn and went toward the lean-to.

Leah Latimer stood outside, her pretty blue eyes wide. "You gonna sleep all day, Danny? And look at that! You haven't even combed your hair!"

Embarrassed, Danny mumbled, "I didn't have anything to comb it with."

"I'll get you my comb," Leah offered. "Pa got it for me at the fort."

She went to a box in a corner of the lean-to, where she located the precious comb. Danny took it and self-consciously brushed the straw out of his hair. *Way to impress the girls, Fortune*, he thought.

"You better go wash up at the creek," Leah said. "Ma's almost got breakfast ready."

Danny washed his face in the cold spring-fed stream, dried his face on his shirt, then went to where the rest were already gathered around a rough-hewn table. "Sorry to be late," he apologized.

Ruth smiled at him. "It's all right. You had a hard day yesterday. Now, you sit down and eat some of these flap-jacks I made."

Danny sat and stared at the large stack on his plate.

"Pitch in!" Latimer said with a grin. "You deserve them after that work you did yesterday."

"Go ahead," Ruth encouraged him. "I'll fix Caleb a little plate, too."

Danny plunged in, cutting the stack with the knife that was beside his plate. There were no forks or spoons in sight.

"Try some of that syrup, boy," Latimer encouraged. "It came from the maple trees on this very farm."

Danny poured syrup liberally over the tender flap-jacks, and, using his knife almost as a weapon, jammed a huge hunk into his mouth. His eyes opened wide. "They're perfect!"

As they finished their hearty breakfast, Joe said, "I think Caleb is better this morning. But it's just as well we got him here. His ma's good for anything that's ailin', animal or human." He leaned back against the homemade oak chair lashed together with rawhide thongs.

"I guess I'll have to take you young folks to the settlement. I don't know if I can do it for a few days, though. Can't afford to leave the family with the Indians on the prowl."

"Oh, that's all right, Mr. Latimer," Dixie reassured him. "There's no hurry."

Danny could tell Joe Latimer was troubled by the look in his eye. "Like I've told you, I've got to get the cabin built and the planting done. Don't know rightly how I'm gonna do all of it." He looked over to where his wife was bending over their son. "I was depending on Caleb. Looks like I'll have to just do it alone now."

Dixie glanced at Danny, and they had one of those moments that twins—even fraternal twins—sometimes have. Danny knew what Dixie was thinking as surely as if she had spoken out loud.

"Mr. Latimer, I know we're city people, but if you'd let us stay on here for a little while, maybe we could help you with the planting and the cabin building. We've seen our share of work." Danny thought back to the long, hard year he and his sister had endured during their time at Plymouth. Had it only been a few short days of their time since they had left?

Latimer stared at them. "Are you sure? Don't you need to get on to meet your father?"

Danny said, "Well . . . we think we know where he's headed. We should be able to catch up with him. Right, Dixie?"

Dixie nodded. "We'll be glad to stay and help all we can. Especially while Caleb's laid up."

Joe Latimer raised his voice. "Ruth, come here a minute!" He waited until his wife came over, then said with a grin, "These two young'uns have agreed to stay until we get the cabin built. They'll even help us with some of the planting. Ain't that grand?"

Ruth smiled and said, "That's real good of you two. We can't afford much, but we'll pay all we can."

"Oh, that's all right," Danny said quickly. "We'd like to do it. We owe your husband for saving us from the bear when he did. Anyway, we'd kind of like to have the experience."

Joe Latimer rubbed his chin, a doubtful look in his eyes. "Well, now, I won't argue with you—raisin' a cabin is an experience, all right. It's hard work, too."

"Oh, we know it, Mr. Latimer. But we're hard workers. You'll see."

Even though Danny and Dixie had helped the Pilgrims to build the settlement at Plymouth, they had had the benefit of being part of a large crew of workers. Now there was no one but the Latimer family to help—and they were short one of their best workers.

Latimer began by putting four stones down and marking the corners. "We'll make it five ax handles wide and about eight ax handles long."

Danny did some quick addition in his head. The result didn't seem like a large enough house for a family.

"That'll be plenty," Ruth agreed. "Let's get started!"

Then the real work began.

All that day and the next, they hauled rocks for the foundation of the house, using a sled that Latimer had constructed from hickory saplings. The blisters on Dixie's and Danny's hands returned and burst again—several times. By the time they had gathered enough rocks to build the house up off the ground, their skin was beginning to callous.

When they had the rocks in place, Caleb was well enough to sit up and eager to have a crutch made so he could limp around.

Once the foundation was complete, Latimer and the twins stood back to admire their work. Danny couldn't remember the last time he'd felt so exhausted.

"We'll use oak for the sills," Latimer announced. "It'll last to eternity. And we'll make the walls of walnut. How many winders you want, Ruth?"

Ruth grew thoughtful. "One is enough. We don't want too many for arrows to pass through."

"I guess that's best. I'd like to have a winder in the back, too, but it'd be too dangerous. I wouldn't feel easy in my mind with a winder there."

"And I ain't wishin' for one," Ruth reminded him. "One will let in a heap of light. I'll scrape a piece of bearskin real thin to stretch over it. And I'll make some shutters so we can close it in the night when it's cold."

Right away, they began cutting lumber. At least, Joe Latimer and Danny did. The women set to work planting while the men chose trees from the vast grove that surrounded them and hewed out logs half an ax handle deep and a quarter wide—huge by modern-day standards. It would take only six logs to wall in a side.

That night, when the others had gone to bed and Latimer and Danny were sitting looking into the fire, Latimer said, "I gotta be honest with you. I just hate to see you working so hard for no money."

In a way, Danny hated it, too, but he was the one who had struck the bargain. Anyway, he knew that the gold coins his great-uncles had given him provided them with all the money he and Dixie would need for this trip—maybe more money than the Latimers could ever hope to see at one time.

Slowly, the pile of logs rose. When at last they were tall enough, Joe turned to Danny. "Now. We got to get the men out and raise the walls."

"Can't we do that ourselves?" Danny asked.

"No. Too much for one man. The neighbors always turn out for a cabin raising once the logs are down. You'll see."

Cabin raising time, Danny soon discovered, was more than just a time to raise a cabin. It was like a holiday for the settlers, who lived scattered all over the Mohawk Valley.

It was up to the owners of the prospective cabin to furnish the food for the big event. For days before, Ruth, Dixie, and Leah worked hard to prepare everything— two deer, corn bread, and a variety of pies. When the time came, the Latimers and the twins were worn out, yet happy to see the yard full of men and women and young adults.

The young people of the valley seemed especially interested in Danny and Dixie.

"Be careful," Leah whispered to Danny. "Some of these boys might see your sister as a possible bride."

Danny was horrified. "But she's only fourteen years old!"

Dixie blushed, obviously overhearing their conversation, and Leah just shook her head. "Ain't uncommon for girls around your age to get married, Dixie. My best friend, Ouida, got married last year. She's fifteen."

"That's not for me," Dixie replied. "I'm too young for marriage. Anyway, we'll need to be moving on soon to find our father."

Danny quickly noticed one very pretty young girl with long, curly black hair. Her name was Susan, and she made a point of standing where he could visit with her.

Caleb hobbled over on his crutch and whispered to Danny, "I wouldn't have much to do with Susan, was I you."

Danny stared at him. "Why? What's wrong with her?"

"There's nothin' *wrong* with her," Caleb grinned. "But she's got a feller named William Baxter who's right jealous." He grinned. "William's busted up several good-sized boys. Including me. I gotta admit I had my eyes on Susan—until William closed them for me."

Danny had already noticed the hulking young man whom Caleb pointed out. William appeared to be a couple of years older than himself and a good deal stronger.

"Well, he doesn't have to worry about me," Danny said. "I'm not going to stick around."

The men put in a hard day's work notching logs and lifting them into place. When they got too high to lift, they leaned small saplings against the walls and, with an impressive show of strength, rolled them up. At last, the cabin was finished, except the roof.

"We'll do the roof ourselves," Joe Latimer announced. "Time to eat!"

Everyone was ready, and they sat down at the tables Latimer and the other men had lashed together out of saplings. The food was piled high.

To his dismay, Danny found himself sitting by an ever-friendly Susan.

She smiled at him, two dimples appearing in each milky cheek. "Where you from, Danny?" she asked. "You don't seem like a country boy."

"No, I'm not," Danny stuttered. Susan made even Courtney Johnson seem very average. She was easily one of the prettiest girls he'd seen.

It grew dark, and several men pulled out fiddles and a banjo, and music began. As the distant neighbors began to square dance in the open space in front of the new cabin, Danny went to sit beside Caleb.

Just then, Susan walked up, a teasing smile on her

face. "C'mon, Danny. You can't just sit there. Dance with me."

"I don't know how," Danny protested—but Susan grabbed his hands and dragged him out into the open area. He had seen square dancing before but had never tried it. He was too busy watching his feet to pay much attention to anything else—even Susan.

A hand tapped him on the shoulder. "I hate to interrupt, brother, but I need to talk with you for a moment." Dixie led him away from the laughing, twirling dancers. "Caleb told me that William's watching you. Be careful. We can't risk your getting hurt."

Just then, one of the men standing around smoking a pipe interrupted. "Where you kids headed fer?"

Danny decided it would be a good opportunity to see if anyone in the valley had heard of their father. "We don't really know. You see, we're looking for our father. His name's James Fortune, and we thought he might have ended up somewhere in these parts. Ever heard of him?"

The man rubbed his jaw and slowly shook his head. "Nope. Can't say as I've ever even heard the name Fortune before today. Anybody else here know of him?" Several men shook their heads no. "Don't reckon he's here then," the man concluded. "We don't get many strangers—and when we do, we shore know who they are."

Danny was disappointed. "I don't think Dad's in the Mohawk Valley," he whispered to his sister. The fiddles sawed wildly in the background. "Maybe Zacharias and Mordecai should have sent us to another location in the same time period."

"I think you're right," Dixie admitted. "But I don't think we ought to return just yet."

"Okay. Let's talk about it later tonight."

At that moment, Susan strolled over. "Aren't you going to dance with me again, Danny?"

Danny was flattered at her attention—so flattered he tried to ignore the tug on his shirt. A second hard jerk made him turn his head.

Dixie gave him a warning look. "Are you crazy?" she hissed.

"I'm big enough to take care of myself," Danny returned. "Don't worry about me." He turned back to Susan. "Sure, I'd love to dance with you."

The two of them walked back to the small clearing. By now, Danny had gotten the hang of square dancing. It was more fun than any dance he had ever tried—not that he had tried many.

In the middle of the third dance, a huge hand closed around his arm. He wheeled to look up into William's angry eyes. Danny tried to wriggle free, but his arm felt as though it was caught in a steel trap.

"What do you want?" Danny asked.

"I want you to leave my girl alone."

Danny finally jerked his arm loose. He was in no mood to be bullied, especially not in front of such a pretty dancing partner. "Listen, all I'm doing is dancing with her." He glanced at Susan, who was apparently enjoying all this. "Just let us finish this dance, then you can have your turn."

Danny never saw what happened next. He was totally unprepared as a heavy fist caught him on the right cheek. The blow drove him to the hard ground. Before he could get up, William was on him, pummeling his stomach and face.

Danny didn't stand a chance against the hard muscles of the young pioneer. *I'm going to be smashed to a pulp*, he thought fleetingly as another blow caused him to see stars.

In the next instant, a man managed to pull the angry boy away. "What do you mean, settin' on a guest like that!" Joe Latimer demanded, William's neck trapped in one of his powerful hands. "You oughta know better'n that!"

William's father stepped forward. "That's right, son. Now you git."

William turned and left the group, his eyes hard. Danny rolled over—and was amazed to see Susan take William's arm and disappear into the darkness.

"I can't believe it," Danny muttered. He struggled to his feet and turned to William's father. "Don't worry about this, sir. I think Susan was trying to upset your son."

Ruth gave Danny a slight smile as he walked up to her and Dixie. "I'm afraid that there girl's headed for trouble. You're better off lookin' elsewhere."

"She's a flirt!" Dixie added fiercely.

"Come with me, Danny," Ruth instructed, "and I'll put some cold presses on them eyes of yours so they won't swell up so bad."

But despite Ruth's efforts, Danny's eyes did swell. By bedtime that night, he could hardly see out of them. They were closed to mere slits.

"Don't worry about it, Danny," Dixie whispered. "Your eyes will be fine in no time."

Danny was embarrassed. "I should have listened to you, Dix. Let's get out of here. We're not going to find Dad in this place."

Dixie hesitated, then said, "Let's give it another day or two. Then if we don't learn something, we can go back and start from square one."

"All right," he conceded. "I have to admit—I'd hate to go back with my eyes looking like this. But as soon as the swelling goes down, I'm ready to leave this valley and look somewhere else for Dad."

5

When Danny got up the next morning, he could barely see out of his eyes—they were still swollen almost shut. In fact, his entire face had turned hideous shades of purple and green.

"You can't go back to the present like this!" Dixie exclaimed. "We'll have to wait until you get better."

Danny had to agree. Actually, he was too ashamed to let Mordecai and Zacharias see him in this condition—and he didn't want to have to explain the whole ridiculous situation to them.

Late that afternoon, he and Dixie got their first look at the valley settlers' dreaded enemy. Danny was sitting on a log helping Dixie shell peas when, without a sound, an Indian man suddenly emerged from the wood and started across the field. Alarmed, Danny called out, "Mr. Latimer! Mr. Latimer! There's an Indian coming!"

Latimer immediately dropped the saw he was using and snatched up his gun, then glanced across the field.

To Danny's surprise, he set the gun back down and grinned. "Aw, that's just Little Horse," he said.

"How, Little Horse," Latimer said as the man approached.

Little Horse raised one hand in greeting. "How," he replied.

51

"Meet Danny and Dixie Fortune," Latimer said, waving his hand toward the twins.

Little Horse turned to look at them and said solemnly, "How."

Danny was not impressed by Little Horse. Unlike the Indians he had known in Plymouth, Little Horse smelled—a reek so strong it had already overpowered every other smell. *If ever water touched him,* Danny thought, *it's been when he was wading through a creek.*

Little Horse wore leggings and a battered skirt of fringed and beaded deerskin. His weathered hunting shirt was now so greasy that it was impossible to tell what its original color had been. A felt hat pierced with the stem of a basswood leaf topped off the tattered outfit.

"How," Little Horse said again before sitting down on a stump.

"We don't have much to offer you, Little Horse. Milk suit you?" Latimer asked.

"Fine," said the Indian, slapping his hand on his stomach.

Danny threw a glance at Dixie, who looked a little queasy. Wordlessly, she went over to the spring, retrieved the jug of milk, and poured a cup for Little Horse, who drank it noisily, then belched his approval.

Rubbing his stomach, Little Horse turned to Joe Latimer. "Bad Injuns come."

A dark cloud passed over Latimer's face. "Where are they comin' from?"

"That way," Little Horse pointed. "One day journey. Maybe less. We leave now."

Latimer didn't waste any time. He threw his saw aside and ran toward the cabin, calling, "Ruth! Gather up some things. We've got to go to the stockade!"

The twins stared at each other in shock, then rose.

"What is happening, Mr. Latimer?" Dixie asked.

"The Seneca are on the raid," he answered. "We've got to get you to the stockade. They'll be sending all the men out to fight. It ain't safe to stay here."

Ruth Latimer was ready almost instantly. "We'll have to take Caleb in the wagon. He can't ride a horse yet."

The party was on its way only moments later. Caleb had been installed in the wagon bed with his sister and the twins. Little Horse pressed uncomfortably close to the twins as he, too, climbed into the back of the wagon, his smell seemingly stronger than before. Joe and Ruth Latimer rode in the front.

Because of its urgency, the trip to the stockade was rough and jolting, and Danny was relieved when they finally reached the stockade. Other settlers were pouring in, frantic to get into the safety of the twelve-foot pointed log walls before the Seneca attacked.

After they climbed out of the wagon, Danny helped Caleb hobble inside. The stockade was much smaller than Danny had expected. The bark sheath roofs of its buildings hung only a foot above his head, and the ground was packed hard and empty of plants. The place was full of people.

Joe Latimer stopped to have a word with Ruth. "I'll be back soon. I doubt it'll be much of a raid, but it's best you be here." He kissed her, then joined the men outside who were forming a loose regiment.

"It's crowded in here, isn't it?" Dixie observed as soon as the men had left. She, Danny, and Leah were fixing a resting place for Caleb, whose leg was still bothering him.

"If you think so now," Leah began with a frown, "just wait till all the settlers are here. There won't be room to sit or stand."

Unfortunately, Leah was right. The next two days were far from comfortable. The twins had lived in closer quarters on the *Mayflower*, but it was harder for them to accept the crowded life at the stockade, knowing that open countryside was just beyond its walls. The tiny buildings quickly turned into saunas—even the church, which was made of stone so it would keep cool, grew so hot people preferred to sit outside in the dusty common area.

More frustrating for Danny was the lack of anything to do. The only exercise was to walk around the outside of the fort, keeping within five feet of the stockade walls for safety. The woods and fields near the stockade were strictly off limits—they might be cover for an Indian. Even a visit to the closest farms was too risky. He and Dixie were thoroughly bored.

"I'm ready to use the Recall Unit," Dixie sighed.

"I know what you mean," Danny said, "but they'd miss us if we disappeared now. Anyway, I think we should wait until Mr. Latimer gets back. I want to be sure he's okay."

The men returned the next day. Since it was Sunday, they had a celebration service that afternoon.

The people gathered together on the rough benches in the cramped stone church. In the front, on a high platform, stood a white-haired man. He had a thin face, and his eyelids stretched tight over his eyes.

He began to pray, "O God Almighty, Father of our Lord Jesus Christ, hear us. . . ."

The prayer touched on the general events around the stockade, then became more specific.

"We are praying now for Mary Wolber. She's just fifteen years old, yet she's going with a soldier from Fort Dayton. He's a Massachusetts man, and I've heard he's married. God, stop that thing right where it stands if that is so."

Danny cast an amazed glance at Dixie. "He doesn't mess around when he prays, does he?" he whispered.

The prayer went on. "Almighty God, you've brought us good crops. Keep them coming! We give thanks, too, for the good lambing we've had this year. Particularly for Joe Wellingham, who's had eleven couples lambed from his twelve ewes—a record in this country."

Dixie leaned in toward Danny. "And he certainly keeps God well informed about what's going on."

Danny grinned but nudged her with his elbow. "We'd better pay attention," he said.

When the prayer was finally done, the preaching started. Little Horse sat right in the front row, saying "amen" so often that the preacher finally had to say, "My dear brother Little Horse, will you please hold your amens so I can get a word in?"

Little Horse promised but was unable to keep it, he grew so excited. Danny snorted in disgust, thinking, *Anyone who is that noisy in church is just trying to get attention. How pathetic!*

After the lengthy service was over, Danny and Dixie went to see what Latimer was planning to do. They found him standing beside Caleb. "Guess we'll stay overnight," he said. "If we left now, it'd be dark before we got home, and there still might be some Indians around."

Cautiously, Danny asked, "Did you catch up with the Seneca, then, Mr. Latimer?"

The man's eyes grew hard, and he shrugged. "Yep, we caught 'em—some of 'em are staying right where we found 'em."

"So you killed them?"

"That's right, boy." An odd look came to Latimer's eyes, and he hurried on. "We'll leave early tomorrow morning. In the meantime, let's rest up."

As Danny walked the stockade, he found himself being followed by Little Horse, who insisted on sharing the full story of his conversion. Danny disliked being around Little Horse so much that he finally said, "I'm going for a walk around the fort."

Little Horse looked at him in surprise. "Not good, brother." He shook his head. "Bad Indians still outside."

But Danny, anxious to escape, strode out the front gate. *I'll just stretch my legs a little before bed*, he told himself. *These crowds are driving me crazy.*

He walked into the grove of trees over to the west, where the welcoming sound of a little brook greeted him. Hot and thirsty from the too warm summer day, he hurried toward the sound until he stood on the bank of the small creek. Lowering to his knees, he put his lips to the cool water. Suddenly, a strong hand gripped the back of his neck.

"Hey!" Danny protested as his head was twisted violently around. Shocked, he stared into the eyes of the most terrible-looking Indian he'd ever seen! He opened his mouth to call out for help, but the Indian, whose face was striped with red-and-green war paint, hit him with the flat side of the ax he carried in his hand.

The world exploded in flashing colors and lights, then disappeared into a black hole.

When Danny awoke, he had a splitting headache. Worse still, he realized his hands were tied and he was slung on his stomach across the back of a horse. When he twisted his head, he saw the red, naked back of an Indian in front of him. The small pony they rode traveled in short, jerky steps, joggling Danny up and down, almost cutting off his air supply. There was no way he could cry for help, and no reason to think he would live to see help if he could cry out.

The ride seemed to go on forever, and Danny grew nauseous. At last the horse stopped, and he was jerked to the ground. He sprawled on the dirt, rolled over, and looked up into the cruel face of his captor. The Indian scowled and, without warning, kicked him in the side.

The kick drove the air out of Danny's lungs, but guessing what was meant by it, he scrambled to his feet.

He saw that he was in an Indian camp—a very small one. There were several crude huts and a few teepees. All around, he was met by the unfriendly eyes of the men and women and children who had come to stare at him.

Danny tried to control the fear that ran through him. He had heard stories of the horrible things Indians did to their captives—how they tortured them and did things like pull their fingernails out. His knees felt weak as his captor spoke angrily to those around him.

A cry of agreement went up, and Danny was seized by many hands. He clamped his lips together as they struck at him and shoved him around. One even spit at him.

Then another gray-haired Indian, tall in spite of his years, cried out. Everyone stopped and waited.

That must be the chief, Danny thought. Unfortunately, the chief's expression appeared to be just as cruel as that of the man who had brought him. *But I doubt I'll be getting any help from him.*

After a hurried discussion, the Indian who had captured Danny grabbed him and hauled him to a tree, where he tied Danny's hands behind his back so he was bound securely to the tree. The man then put his face close to Danny's, glared at him, hissed something incomprehensible, and turned and walked away.

For the next hour, the people of the village, especially the younger ones, came by to stare at Danny. Most taunted him and tried to frighten him—one went so far as to hold up a steel knife, draw it across the air, and point it right at him.

They're going to kill me, Danny thought. *I know they*

are! And there's nothing I can do about it . . . except . . .
He remembered the Recall Unit, still cold against his
chest. He could use it to escape—but if he did, it would
mean stranding Dixie in the past.

Maybe I could come back for her again, Danny rea-
soned. *But if it didn't work and I couldn't. . . .* He felt sick.
He knew his mother would be devastated if his sister
were suddenly missing, too. And he would never be able
to forgive himself. *I've got to escape!*

All evening he stood tied to the tree, his hands behind
him. With effort, he eventually managed to sit down and
ease his weak legs. By now, he was so thirsty he would
have given anything for a drink of water, but no one paid
any attention to him.

The Indians were cooking something over a fire, but
he was too thirsty to be tempted by it. He longed for one
sip from the bag they passed around and drank from.
Finally, as the night grew darker, the Indians grew sleepy
and retired to their small huts. The one who had captured him, however, came over, the firelight gleaming on
his dark eyes.

"Tomorrow you die."

Danny was shocked. "You speak English! Please! Let
me go! You can get a ransom for me." Danny was glad
he had thought to give Dixie the gold coins for safe-
keeping. Maybe she could buy him back!

But either the Indian wasn't interested in a ransom,
or he didn't understand. "Tomorrow you die," he repeated menacingly. He pulled out his knife and placed
it against Danny's throat, pressing the cold steel so close
that Danny did not dare move. The Indian laughed and

put the knife back in its sheath, then turned and walked away.

Alone, Danny sat, his hands tied so tightly behind him they had lost all feeling. His tongue was swollen in his mouth, and his lips were dry as dust. Overhead the skies were glittering and bright with what seemed to be millions of stars. *This will probably be the last time I'll ever see them*, he thought sadly.

All through the long dark hours, Danny sat and thought about his family, wondering what it would be like to die, dreading what might come in the morning and the torture that they might put him through. Finally, he said simply, "God, you know where I am and all the trouble I'm in. Please help me. Help me to get loose."

The stars overhead glowed with a cold light, and the wind began to howl. To Danny, it seemed that God had forgotten him, and he was terrified.

6

That night felt like it went on forever. Danny gazed apprehensively across the clearing toward the warriors, who were stretched out in front of the dying fire. It was a warm night, but the thought of what waited for him in the morning caused a cold sweat to break out on his forehead. He tried desperately to think of some way to break loose, but the rawhide thongs that bound his hands were too strong.

Somewhere far off a wolf was howling. A lonesome, mournful call. Then all was quiet.

Suddenly, a slight sound attracted Danny's attention. Something was moving off to his right—or so he thought. Danny squinted his eyes, trying to peer into the darkness, and decided it was nothing. He strained against the thongs, knowing it was hopeless. Then—he spotted a slight movement in the nearby trees.

Something's out there! he thought. At any other time he might have been frightened, thinking it was a wolf or a mountain lion. Now he didn't care. *Even if it is something dangerous, maybe it will take a few of these warriors with me.*

The Indians sleeping in front of the fire did not move as a faint shadow slipped in and out of the range of Danny's sight. He waited, not daring to breathe. Someone was creeping up behind him!

For one moment, Danny had the urge to yell. Perhaps an Indian from the camp was playing a trick on him. But he kept his lips closed and sat perfectly still.

A few moments passed. Then something touched his hands!

In spite of himself, Danny jerked. There came a whisper so quiet only he could possibly hear it. "Hush!"

He felt something cold touch his wrists. In an instant his hands were free!

He tried to lurch forward, but the person had a firm grip on his hands.

"Be still!" the voice warned. Danny forced himself to remain absolutely still. "Now, be very quiet. No noise or we die."

Danny felt the hands holding his loosen their grip. He pulled his own hands forward, rubbing his wrists to restore feeling, then slowly got to his feet, careful not to make a sound. Heart pounding, he kept his eyes fixed on the warriors lying asleep in front of the fire. Then he turned toward the shadowy figure.

Danny's eyes were so used to the light of the fire that at first he could not see against the total blackness.

"We go!" the shadow indicated as it stepped backward. "Be very still, brother. No noise."

The figure seemed to fade into the dark, and Danny put each foot down as carefully as if he were walking on broken glass. If one snap of a twig reached the Indians at the fire, he would be dead. Slowly, agonizingly, he followed the figure into the darkness.

As they reached the line of trees where the light of the campfire was barely visible, a hand touched his arm.

"Who are you?" Danny whispered when he dared.

"Little Horse."

Little Horse! Danny could not believe it. The Indian that he had disliked so much had come to save him!

"How did you—"

"No talk. Come."

Danny felt the hand tighten on his arm, then Little Horse moved ahead, holding lightly to Danny to guide him through the dark. The man must have had eyes like a cat because Danny could see nothing. Several times he would have walked right into the trunks of huge trees, but the Indian guided him around them.

They reached a large clearing, and just as they stepped inside into the clear light of the moon, a dog appeared on the other side. Danny and Little Horse stopped abruptly—but it was too late. The animal began a series of shrill barks.

"Come," said Little Horse, breaking into a dead run.

Danny stumbled after him, running across the open field, thankful that they were out of the woods. But he knew the warriors' pursuit would be quick. They ran across the field, splashed through a creek, then entered a small forest of saplings and scrub timber.

As Little Horse made his way, trees slapped backward, catching Danny in the face. He threw his hands up and stumbled behind, running as hard as he could. Soon his breath was coming harder, but Little Horse said, "Run! No time!"

Danny knew it meant death to stop. He could picture

the terrible face of the Indian who had captured him, and he shuddered.

He couldn't tell how far they had run. His breath was completely gone, coming first in little gasps, then in great choking sobs. Little Horse had to drag him on by a firm grasp on his arm. At last, Danny's rescuer pulled him down beside a hulking dead tree that had fallen and formed a hiding place between it and a bank.

"Quiet!" Little Horse warned as Danny drew in another rattling breath. "Be very still!"

Frightened, Danny forced himself to draw in smaller gasps of air. He felt as if he would suffocate.

Danny tried to listen for pursuers, but his ears were not nearly as good as those of Little Horse. Even so, after a moment, he thought he heard the faint sound of someone coming through the brush. *They'll find us!*

"He come now," Little Horse whispered fiercely.

"Can't we run away?" Danny gasped.

"White boy no run like Indian. We wait. You rest."

For perhaps thirty minutes they did lie there, and Danny was able to regain his breath. Then Little Horse said, "Come. Sun come soon." They left their hiding place and plunged across a valley and up a steep hill. As they cleared the crest, a thin line of light appeared in the east.

"They find our trail soon," Little Horse observed seriously. "Run fast. Jesus God, He help us."

Danny looked into the face of the Indian, remembering how he had looked down on him and doubted his faith. "Thanks, Little Horse, for coming to help me."

The man grinned broadly, revealing two rows of yellowed teeth. "We brothers, Danny. Brothers in Jesus Christ." Then he said, "Come. We go home now."

They began the trip back to the Latimers' farm, Little Horse cutting a zigzag path through the forest. At one point, they walked upstream in a small river for at least a mile before stepping out. Danny knew this was to wipe out any sign of their path.

When they had left the stream, Little Horse said, "Now we go straight. We find Latimer cabin soon." He broke into a trot, and Danny followed. This time, he was able to keep up—Little Horse was deliberately slowing his pace.

The sun rose higher and the earth began to warm. Before they had gone more than two miles, Danny recognized a hill.

"I know that place!" he said. "We're not far from the Latimers'!"

"Yes. We go on," Little Horse said. He quickly glanced over his shoulder and added, "Them bad Indians come."

They began to run again and had gone less than half a mile when Little Horse spoke again, more urgently this time. "They come now! Run—hard!"

Danny cast one look back as they broke into a headlong run. A warrior emerged from the bush—the Indian who had captured him! He appeared to be alone, but even at this distance, Danny could see the murderous hatred on his face. Desperate with fear, he followed Little Horse as fast as his heavy feet would fly.

The only sound came from the slap of his shoes as they hit the ground. They passed a familiar tree—they were now no more than half a mile from the Latimers' cabin—but it was still half a mile too far.

Glancing over his shoulder, Danny noted their pursuer had cut the distance in half. He had a bow in hand and would soon be within shooting range. Danny willed his legs to pump faster.

Ahead of him, Little Horse stopped. "You go on," he ordered, pulling a knife from his belt.

"But he's got a bow!" Danny gasped.

"Yes. You go now."

Danny ran with all the strength he had left. He topped the familiar hill overlooking the Latimer cabin. *I can make it!* he thought.

A sharp cry caused him to turn. His would-be captor was racing toward him, a hatchet in hand. Little Horse was nowhere to be seen.

He knows he can catch me! Danny thought wildly. He flew down the hill, yelling, "Joe! Joe!" There was no sound from the cabin. Danny felt sick.

The sound of the warrior's footsteps was nearer now. The Latimers were probably still at the fort—no doubt searching for him. There was no hope. Even if Danny made it to the cabin, the Indian would have him at his mercy.

Danny was afraid to turn and look as the footsteps neared. The angry grunt behind him told him it would be over soon.

He whirled. The warrior's sweaty body gleamed in the morning sunlight, his face twisted with hatred. His eyes sparked as he raised his hatchet to bring it down—on Danny's head!

Desperately, Danny threw himself to one side. He felt rather than saw the Indian sail past him. He tried to scramble away, but the warrior stopped, wheeled, and was on him like a huge cat.

Danny felt a cruel hand clutch his hair and jerk his head upright. The hatchet flashed in the sun as the Indian raised it for the deadly stroke.

I wish I could see my family one last time, Danny thought, surprised he felt no fear.

Then, suddenly, the Indian stiffened—a fraction of a second later, Danny heard the muffled sound of a rifle exploding.

The warrior slid to the ground, a small blue hole in his right temple. His limbs twitched and slowly stretched out.

Danny stared at the fallen Indian, then looked toward the cabin. Ruth Latimer had stepped out of the cabin, her husband's musket in her hand. She dropped it and came toward Danny, and he ran straight into her open arms.

Leah and Dixie came out of the cabin, their faces pale.

"Danny!" Dixie cried. He gave her a limp smile.

"It's all right, Danny," Ruth said, hugging him hard. "You're safe now."

He began to shake. Now that it was over, the terror of the moment nearly overcame him. His legs felt as weak as water.

"Here, sit down," Ruth said gently. She helped him down onto one of the benches in front of the cabin.

"Where . . . where's Mr. Latimer?" he asked.

"He's out with a search party looking for you," Ruth answered. Then she stared at him in wonder. "How did you get away from the Seneca? They had you captured, didn't they?"

"Yes. And Little Horse . . . he . . ." Suddenly Danny remembered the man who had freed him, and jumped to his feet.

"I've got to go to him!" He broke into a run. "I think he's been hurt!" He raced up the hill, past the dead warrior, back up to the crest, and stopped. Little Horse's still form lay on the ground.

"Little Horse!" he cried, running to his friend's side.

An arrow pierced Little Horse's abdomen, but he was alive. Falling on his knees, Danny gently raised the Indian's head, paying no attention now to his rank smell.

"Little Horse," he whispered. "Can you hear me?"

The man's eyes slowly opened, and he smiled. "You safe now?" he whispered feebly.

"Yes. I'm all right. Mrs. Latimer shot the Seneca," he said. Then he added, "Are you hurt bad?" He didn't need to hear the answer to know it. He could see that Little Horse's eyes were already glazing over.

Little Horse slapped his stomach with his hand and grinned. "Fine." Then his hand fell away, and he whispered, so faintly that Danny could barely hear him, "Little Horse . . . he go to Jesus now. . . ."

Tears ran down Danny's face. "Please don't die!" he begged.

Little Horse focused on Danny again. "Little Horse go to Jesus . . . me wait for you."

The man's head fell to one side. His chest sank in, and he was gone.

When the others found him, Danny was sitting in the dirt, holding the dead body of his friend, Little Horse of the Iroquois.

7

Danny stood silently beside the grave of Little Horse as the minister spoke. He had never felt more terrible in his life. *How could I have misjudged him, God? Am I really that shallow?*

Only Dixie seemed to understand his sadness at the death of his friend. "Danny, I think it's time to move on," she announced after the funeral.

"You're right. We're obviously not going to find Dad around here. Let's get away as soon as we can."

Leaving proved to be fairly simple. They asked Joe Latimer to bring them to the fort, saying they would leave from there to find their father.

When they arrived at the fort, they said their good-byes to the Latimers, then found passage on a wagon train leaving for the east. They wanted to travel to a settlement where no one knew them before slipping away—that way, their disappearance would be less likely to draw any unwanted attention.

As soon as possible, they walked into the woods. "Ready?" Danny asked, reaching inside his shirt for the Recall Unit. At Dixie's nod, he pressed the button.

Instantly a heavy green fog descended, and the earth began to sway. In another second, they were back in the laboratory of Zacharias Fortune.

"You're back soon. Did you find any sign of your father?" Zacharias asked before they could even step out of the Chrono-Shuttle.

"No," Danny said. "We didn't find a trace of him in the Mohawk Valley. We need to try another location—one closer to George Washington, maybe."

"Exactly," Mordecai said. Evidently he had entered the lab soon after the twins had left for the valley. "James would have wanted to be near George Washington. Why on earth did you choose to send the kids to the Mohawk Valley, Zacharias? George wouldn't have been there! I knew I should have been in the lab to help oversee the send-off." Mordecai gave his twin a withering glare.

"Zacharias, change the location finder on the Chrono-Shuttle to Mount Vernon."

Sheepishly, Zacharias hurried to comply. He tinkered with the settings, then stepped back. "Do you want to freshen up or anything before you go?"

Danny glanced at Dixie. "No," he said. "We want to get this over with."

"All right, then." Zacharias pushed the button, and they were quickly overtaken by the now-familiar sensation of vibration and falling.

This time Danny was not as nervous. They reappeared near a dirt road leading past some large fields.

"It's weird, but I guess I'm getting used to this time-travel thing." Danny looked around and added, "I don't see anything that looks like a plantation. But we'll just follow that road. Someone will be able to tell us where to go."

They had not walked more than a quarter of a mile when they saw a group of slaves working in a field. A short, heavy, bearded man on a horse was watching them, and he watched as Danny and Dixie came toward him. "How are ye?" he said in a friendly voice as the pair approached.

Danny said, "Fine, sir. We're looking for the home of Colonel Washington."

"Ye be not far from it," the man replied. "Take this road less than five miles, take a right, and ye'll be there soon."

"Thank you," Danny said.

"I guess I'm a little afraid of meeting George Washington," Dixie confessed as the twins made their way down the road. "I mean, he's the 'Father of our Country'! And we're going to meet him."

Danny shrugged. "It's exciting, all right. But I'd rather see Dad than George Washington any day."

He changed the subject. "Dixie, I think something's wrong with me."

Dixie looked at him quickly. "Why? Don't you feel well?"

"Oh, physically I feel fine. But I made a terrible mistake."

Dixie knew what he meant. "Oh. You're still thinking about Little Horse."

"Yes." Danny shook his head sadly. "I didn't like him, Dixie. I thought he was a hypocrite—and all the time, he was a great Christian. How could I have been so wrong?"

"We all make mistakes, Danny," Dixie sounded thoughtful. "I didn't like him either. He was dirty and he smelled bad, and he wasn't like . . . he just wasn't like . . ." She hesitated. "He wasn't like us, you know?"

"So all Christians have to be like us, Dix? No, that's not right. We both should know better than that." He kicked up some dust and concluded, "I'm going to be more careful in the future about judging people. Just because someone doesn't smell right or look right or seem right, I'm not going to put him down. He might turn out to be as great a person as Little Horse." He shook his head sadly. "He gave his life for me, Dixie. Not many people would do that. He even said he would be waiting for me in heaven."

Dixie gave Danny a quick pat on the shoulder. "I know it's sad, but just think—when you get to heaven, you'll see Little Horse there, waiting for you with a smile on his face. I bet he'll still be patting his stomach and saying, 'Fine!' "

Danny had to smile at the thought.

They reached the turn-off and headed to the right. Before long, Danny said, "Look, there's a river over there. I'll bet it's the Potomac. That means Mount Vernon should be nearby. I know at least that much history."

As they rounded a bend, a large, beautiful house with big white pillars appeared.

"That's Mount Vernon all right," Dixie said excitedly. "I recognize it from the pictures I've seen. Isn't it amazing to think that people can still visit this place in our time?"

The estate's immaculately kept green lawns seemed to go on forever. Away and off to one side were several smaller buildings, probably slave quarters. Danny looked eagerly around, hoping to catch a glimpse of the owner of the house. Some men were working in the yard off to one side, but he didn't see anyone who looked like George Washington.

"This place is a lot larger than I expected. I guess we'll have to ask for Washington if we want to find him," Dixie said. "Danny, could you do the talking?"

"Sure," he agreed.

But as they walked up the long driveway to the house, Danny felt his heart thumping. He was more nervous than he wanted to admit when he approached the front door and knocked.

The door opened and a tall black man peered out. "Yes," he said. "What can I do for you?"

"We . . . we'd like to see Colonel Washington," Danny stammered.

"You'll find him down at the stables," the man answered.

The twins turned and walked away from the house, and Danny whispered, "You're right, Dixie. It does feel really odd to be here. But we've got to try every possible way of finding Dad. It isn't—"

"Oh! Look at all the horses," Dixie interrupted, pointing in the direction of a large barn that rose up against the sky. "That's got to be the stable over there."

They approached the field and saw two men standing

beside a horse. One stood by while a stable hand saddled the animal, and Danny nudged his sister. "That's him, Dixie! The tall man!"

"Yes. You couldn't miss him, even if he does look a lot younger than in the paintings I've seen."

Danny said, "Yeah, well, those were done after the Revolution. That won't come for a long time yet. He's only twenty-three years old right now." He took a deep breath. "Well, no way to do this but just do it. C'mon."

They advanced to the split-rail fence that bordered the field and waited while the groom saddled the horse. As soon as it was ready, George Washington took the reins and started to swing into the saddle. Then he noticed Danny and Dixie.

"That'll be all, Henry," he said, approaching the twins, the reins in his left hand.

At six three or six four, George Washington was every bit as tall and strong looking as Danny had first thought. He had blunt features, including a broad nose and a heavy forehead, and a kind expression. His pale blue eyes looked inquiringly at the pair. "Good morning," he said. "What can I do for you two young people?"

"We are hoping to be able to work for you, Colonel Washington, sir," Danny responded.

Washington cocked one eyebrow. "Work? Why would you be looking for work here?"

"Our father's missing, and we're here without family," Danny began. "My sister and I need a way to make a living, and we thought you might have something to do around Mount Vernon. We're young, I know, but we'd be willing to work hard for almost nothing."

Washington inspected them for a moment, then shook his head. "I'm not sure that will answer," he said quietly. "However, if you have no place to go, we can do something about that. My manager has a big house and a wife, but his children are all gone. I'll speak to him if you like. You can stay there awhile, and we can talk about what to do with you."

"Oh, that would be wonderful!" Dixie exclaimed. "Thank you so much, sir."

Washington nodded, smiled, and mounted his horse. "Follow me, and I'll take you over to meet Mrs. Miles. She and her husband Charles have been with me a long time. I'm sure they can find a place for you."

The twins followed Washington as he walked his horse slowly away from the barn, and soon they were standing in front of the house. A woman of about fifty with a round red face and a pleasant smile came out to meet them.

Washington greeted her. "Mrs. Miles, these young people need a place to stay. Could you and your husband keep them until we find something for them?"

Mrs. Miles beamed. "Why, certainly, Colonel," she said. "You leave them right here with me. This big old house has been too empty since the last of my children left."

"That settles it, then," Washington said with a warm laugh. "Mrs. Miles will take care of you. We'll find time to talk soon."

He wheeled his horse away, and Danny had time only to say, "Thank you very much, Colonel," before Washington rode away with a wave of his hand.

"Come into the house. You must be hungry. Got plenty in the kitchen," Mrs. Miles said, shooing them toward the door. "What might your names be, now, and where did you come from?"

She led them into the house, keeping up a constant stream of cheerful chatter. By the time she had set food before them, Danny and Dixie had introduced themselves and told their story.

"Why, there's plenty to do on a place like this," their hostess said. "I'm sure Colonel Washington will allow you to stay."

Danny and Dixie looked at each other and drew sighs of relief.

When they had finished, Mrs. Miles led them upstairs to their rooms. "We've got so many empty rooms here, you can take your pick."

She left them to settle in to the rooms they had chosen. After sleeping in the Latimers' barn, the simple rooms furnished only with a bed and chest of drawers looked almost luxurious. Each had a single window.

"Look at this, Dixie!" Danny said, examining his bed. "The box spring is made out of rope. But it's got a thick feather bed on top. Let's take a look at yours."

Dixie's was exactly like it. "Well," she said as she moved to look out her window. "We're off to a good start. At least we've got a place here at Mount Vernon where we can stay for a while."

"Yeah. Now, if only someone around here has heard of Dad."

"It hardly seems like a week since we got here, does it, Danny?" Dixie asked one morning.

"No, it doesn't. And even though we really haven't had a chance to find out anything about Dad, we've sure learned a lot about a Virginia planter's life. I was really surprised that most of the house slaves aren't black."

"I know what you mean. I guess in these parts they usually have to work in the tobacco fields." Dixie fingered the apron covering her dress. "What do you think of Colonel Washington?"

"So far he seems great—nothing at all like Mordecai and Zacharias thought he would be."

Dixie laughed. "At first I kept my eyes open for Martha Washington, too, but I finally remembered that she didn't marry Washington until 1759."

"It seems weird to think that we know what's going to happen in Washington's life before he does. I mean, we could tell him all kinds of things about his family—even that there will be a revolution and he will become the first American president." Danny shook his head at the thought. It was mind-boggling.

"Anyway, I guess Mordecai will have to rethink his theories about history when we tell him how nice Washington is." He frowned. "But somehow, I don't think even the truth will convince him. Maybe he'll just think we're making it all up to side with our dad."

"Maybe. I guess it doesn't matter so long as *we* know the truth—and so long as we find Dad." Dixie sniffed the air. "Smells like breakfast is ready. Let's get downstairs."

As usual, it was a huge breakfast of battered eggs, baked ham, broiled partridge, corn hoecake, and wheat biscuits. Everything had been made fresh that morning.

"Now, you children eat heartily," Mrs. Miles said with a smile. "You've got a busy day." She poured some cider from a shining silver pitcher for the two, who had discovered that tea and coffee were relatively rare in Virginia at this time.

Mr. Miles had already left for the day, so Mrs. Miles sat down with them. She laughed a lot, revealing teeth black with decay—many were missing.

When Danny had first noticed her mouth, he had been shocked. Obviously there were no dentists in the eighteenth century, or she would have not been in such horrible shape. *Wouldn't she like to know about our modern false teeth?* Danny thought.

Mrs. Miles rattled on happily, and after breakfast the twins went to their work: Dixie to the mansion to help with the cleaning, and Danny to the fields.

By the time Danny arrived, Mr. Miles was already at work, riding up and down the rows to observe as the slaves worked under the warm sun. Danny helped out wherever he was needed, keeping his eyes and ears open for some news of his father.

But it had become clear that no one at Mount Vernon had heard of James Fortune. Later that night, Danny rejoined Dixie to fill her in on his day.

"I still haven't found anyone who knows anything

about Dad," he said. "This is going to be harder than I thought."

Dixie reassured him. "We haven't been here long—we'll find him yet." She looked puzzled about something. "I've been thinking—these Virginians sure are a lot different from the Pilgrims, aren't they?"

"What do you mean?" Danny asked.

"Well, you remember how the Pilgrims were. They worked so hard, and they were always so serious—sometimes too serious. They didn't waste any time." She cocked her head to one side. "But these Virginians, they don't mind wasting time. They love company and other things that distract them from work. There's always a party going on. Remember how earlier this week seven people just dropped in for supper? That would never have happened in Plymouth."

"True," Danny admitted. "And George Washington seems to like visitors most of all. I hope we have a chance to talk to him soon. I'd like to ask him if he's heard of our father. If he hasn't heard of him, then maybe we should just return home."

They got their chance the next day. Colonel Washington came to the Mileses' house at noon when they were eating lunch. After he had joined them at the table, Danny asked, "Colonel Washington, have you ever met someone named James Fortune? He's a relative of mine, and I thought you might have heard of him."

The colonel shook his head. "I'm afraid I have not,

but I will certainly inquire of my acquaintances in the area, particularly the military. They may know of him."

"Thank you, sir. My sister and I would appreciate that." Danny saw another opportunity to ask something he had been wondering about. "Colonel, if you don't mind, I have another question."

Colonel Washington gave a little smile and indicated for Danny to continue.

"I don't understand the reasoning behind the wars England is fighting with the French. What are they all about?"

Washington looked at him kindly, then shook his head. "It's very simple, my boy. This country is a prize. And England and France are fighting to see who will win it." He leaned back. "The French are well established up in Canada and have been for years. But we English are strung out in a thin little line along the coast. Now that the original colonies are filling up, we want to cross over the mountains and occupy the land there. And the French are determined to keep us from it."

"And they're using the Indians to help fight their battles?"

Washington frowned. "They're using them very effectively, I'm afraid. Much better than we are. They serve as scouts, primarily, but also as soldiers. You can't imagine how cruel some of the Indians can be in battle—they can be very dangerous. We English haven't gotten along with them well enough to fight with them against the French. I'm afraid some of our military officers don't trust them—even as scouts."

"What do you think will happen in the end?"

"I think we're going to have a hard time pushing the French out. They've moved deeper and deeper into the Ohio valleys, with no sign of slowing up. It's going to take a lot of military power to beat them." Then he smiled and said, "But, we do have one bit of good news. London has finally realized that we need to have trained full-time soldiers here, and they've ordered two regiments of them sent to Virginia. Two more are going to be raised in this country. General Edward Braddock will be commanding the four regiments. With his leadership, I think we'll be able to do something about this French problem."

Washington talked for a long time about the war with the French. As soon as he was out of the room, Dixie whispered to Danny, "It's too bad we can't tell him how things come out, isn't it?"

"Yeah, but don't even think about it," Danny warned. "You remember what Zacharias and Mordecai said. We can't do anything to change the past because that might change the present."

Dixie grinned. "It's a little like reading the Bible, isn't it? No matter how bad things get for us Christians, we can look at the end in the book of Revelation and see who the winners are." She gazed out the door where George Washington had exited. "And it's almost as nice to know that a fine man like Colonel Washington is going to wind up as the hero of his country."

8

For the next week, Danny and Dixie learned a lot more about life at a big manor house of a wealthy Virginia planter. They were most impressed with the work that needed to be done around the house itself.

All over the mansion, sconces for candles hung on the walls—it was such a job lighting and caring for them it took one slave all day. He molded the candles, polished the sconces and candlesticks, and went around each day replacing the burnt candles with fresh ones infused with the juice of juniper berries. The juice gave the rooms a pleasant, Christmasy odor.

In the kitchen, the cooking was done in a huge fireplace. Out in the yard near the kitchen was a brick baking oven, used chiefly to bake bread and cakes. It took several people working all day just to make the food.

The second week of their stay, Danny and Dixie were asked to serve at a party. As the large group of men and women—the women in full, brightly colored silk dresses—began arriving, the twins and the other servants moved as quietly as ghosts, speaking in low tones to one another and to the guests.

The dishes—and there were many of them—were put out on the table right away. There was a rich vegetable soup, fried oysters, fish chowder, roast goose stuffed with boiled peanuts, sweet potatoes, carrots, and plentiful desserts. The ladies drank coffee after their meal out of cups as large as bowls.

While Danny was waiting on the table, he overheard Colonel Washington talking about tobacco. "It is an economic error of the most vicious kind," Washington said firmly. All the guests turned their attention to him. "I know our whole economy is built on tobacco. And I know it is the only crop that can be sold in Europe for cash on the spot, but it is disastrous for these colonies."

"What do you mean, Colonel?" one of the men seated at the table asked rather defiantly. "Our whole economy, as you point out, is built on tobacco."

"Yes, it is. And because the owners of large estates are able to produce so much tobacco with the labor of slaves and indentured servants, it's ruinous to the small farmer. Tobacco farming, at least the way we presently practice it, produces a permanent class of poverty-stricken people." Washington frowned, his lips turned down severely. "The poor white farmer cannot possibly compete with estate owners."

"Well, you may be right there," the guest admitted. "With tobacco as low as two cents a pound, only a large-scale grower can produce it profitably. But the small farmer—honestly, I don't see how they stay alive."

Finally the party was over, and as Dixie and Danny were leaving to go to the Miles's, Colonel Washington caught them at the door.

"I have a word for you two." He smiled. "I don't know for sure that it means anything, but I have heard this past week of a man called James Fortune."

Danny's heart leaped. "Oh, Colonel Washington!" he exclaimed. "Where is he? Where does he live?"

Washington frowned and shook his head. "I'm not exactly sure. A friend of mine, a tobacco buyer who comes often to Mount Vernon, stopped by yesterday and said he had heard of such a man. Once again, I am not sure he would be a relative of yours."

Danny and Dixie plied him with questions.

Washington held up his hands. "All I know is that he appears to have something to do with the civilian force that's being mustered to assist General Braddock in his military venture."

"General Braddock?" Dixie said. "Is he the one you said is going to lead the force against the French and Indians?"

"He's the one," Washington said. "And I've discovered I'll be going with him."

"Do you think we might go, too, sir?" Danny asked eagerly.

Washington shook his head firmly. "No, I'm afraid not, Danny. It will be a military expedition. There will be no place for a lad of your years."

He put his hand on Danny's shoulder. "I'll try my best to find out what I can about the man, and I'll get word back to you. If I find him, I'll tell him about you."

"Thank you, Colonel," Danny and Dixie said in unison.

On the way back to the Miles's house, Danny said, "Dixie, I've made up my mind—we've got to go. It may be our last chance to find Dad!"

"But how can we go?" she asked. "We can't just take off without the colonel's permission."

They walked along in silence. Just before they reached the house, Danny thought of something. "I have the answer. At least, it's the only one we've got. Let's ask God to somehow fix it so we can go with Colonel Washington."

Dixie was quiet for a minute, then she nodded. "All right, Danny. We'll both pray and believe that God will somehow work it out. But if He chooses not to, we need to go along with His decision."

Danny and Dixie prayed every opportunity they got. They watched carefully as Colonel Washington prepared to leave, giving orders to Mr. Miles and to all of the other workers on the plantation. Yet he said nothing to them.

Finally, on the night before he was to depart, Danny and Dixie were surprised by a knock at the Miles's house.

When Mrs. Miles answered the door, they heard her exclaim, "Why, Colonel Washington! Do come in. What are you doing out this time of the night?"

The twins rose as Colonel Washington entered the main room. He didn't waste any time. "Danny, my servant is ill and won't be able to make the trip with me. I know you're young and haven't had any training as a body servant, but I'm offering you the chance to go with me if you'd like to. You'd see to my uniforms—that sort of thing."

Danny gave Dixie a huge grin. *This couldn't have worked out more perfectly!* he thought. "Yes, Colonel, I would love to go!" he said quickly.

Washington held up his hand and warned, "It'll be dangerous. There'll be fighting. You risk getting hurt, even killed."

Danny nodded stubbornly. "I understand, and I still want to go, Colonel. More than anything."

Dixie looked concerned. "Colonel, may I go, too?"

Colonel Washington studied Dixie for a moment. "Lass, you can't go with the military force, but there is a large company of wood choppers and workers going. Some will feed the officers. Perhaps we can find a place for you with one of those families. Yes, you can come."

Dixie smiled and whispered to Danny, "See. I told you God would answer our prayers."

Danny made a face at her. "No, *I* was the one who told you. Now, let's see what God will do next!"

General Edward Braddock was a foot shorter than George Washington, with more fat than muscle. Danny and Dixie happened to be in Colonel Washington's quarters when he stopped by for the first time. They watched him carefully, and he peered at the two of them from under his shaggy brows, as if he were suspicious of them. He wore a powdered wig under his winged hat, and his uniform blazed with bright decorations and embroidery.

"This young man, Danny Fortune, will be my body servant on the expedition, General Braddock," Colonel Washington said. "And this young lady will help serve the officers. I've made the arrangements."

"Be sure they don't get in the way, Colonel," Braddock responded in a high-pitched voice. "Remember, you're not a part of the military on this expedition. Only an observer."

Washington's lip twitched slightly. "I understand, General. It will be as you say. But I did serve at Fort Necessity, you remember, and have some knowledge of Indians and the way they fight."

The stubborn Englishman's nostrils flared. "You mean that you were *defeated* at Fort Necessity before you even reached your objective."

Washington did not seem troubled by the general's mean-spirited remark. "As you please, General. But I hope to be of service to you this time."

Braddock grunted. "We don't need anything so much as we need good leadership in this country, Washington. I intend to wage a fine European-style war!" The general began to pace up and down the floor, almost speaking to himself. "Orthodox war. No games, no hiding behind trees and jumping out at the enemy like children. These Indians do not know how to fight like men."

Danny looked at Braddock with displeasure as the man delivered a long lecture on the necessity of keeping strict military order. He went on about marching in straight formations and not breaking the line—strategies that Danny's history course had told him would be ineffective against the Indians, who preferred to ambush their enemies. At last, the general left, slamming the door behind him. Washington looked at his two guests.

"He never was an easy man to deal with, but he is one of the most experienced soldiers in the British army. A long-time career officer. So we'll see what he can do against the Indians."

Danny asked carefully, "But, sir, what if the Indians hide in bushes and trees and ambush the army?"

Washington gave him a sharp glance. "Exactly what I've been wondering. But surely it won't come to that. We'll see."

That very day, the troops began assembling. "I want to learn all I can from the general," Washington stated to one of his aides. "These troops are hand-picked from England. They've been unbeatable on the Continent, and General Braddock says they'll sweep the French out of the West. He must have his chance."

"Yes, sir," replied the aide, a young man named Brinkley. "But it's different here. I'm not sure those battle tactics will work."

Washington shook his head. "It doesn't matter. We have to give him his chance."

Colonel Washington found a place for Dixie with an Irish family named Muldoon. The husband and the son were to be woodcutters and horse handlers for the army, while Mrs. Muldoon was to do some of the cooking for the officers. She welcomed Dixie with open arms.

"Ah, me dear," she said with a broad smile. "It's glad

I am to have you! I'll need all the help I can get to fill the gullets of these lobsterbacks!" She put Dixie right to work.

Meanwhile, Danny followed Colonel Washington from dawn until dark. There was so much to do that he barely had time to ask the colonel if he had learned more about James Fortune.

"No, my boy," Colonel Washington answered with a harried look on his face. "You can ask around as well as I. If I do hear anything, I'll report to you."

Danny did ask almost everyone. But no one knew of a man named Fortune.

The war preparations went on. The cannons were assembled, along with soldiers, horses, feed, and all the other things necessary to support an army.

On the night before they were due to leave, the twins sat staring into a fire. Danny had been quiet most of the day.

"I know what you're thinking," Dixie said.

Danny looked up. "What?"

"You're thinking about Little Horse again, aren't you?"

Danny looked back into the fire and nodded. "I can't help it, Dixie. It was my fault he died, and I can't forgive myself. I guess I'll always feel guilty about it."

The fire crackled, and Dixie was silent for a moment. Then she put her hand on Danny's and said, "Danny, you know Jesus died for all of our sins. He doesn't keep track of them and bring them up before us. You've asked God to forgive you for misjudging Little Horse, haven't you?"

"At least a dozen times."

"And if you asked me a dozen times to forgive you, I'd think you didn't believe me if I'd already said you were forgiven." She squeezed Danny's hand. "Don't you think God is better than I am?"

Danny shot her a startled glance. "Why, I never thought of it like that," he admitted. He paused for a moment before adding quietly, "I guess you're right. Once God forgives us, it's done forever."

Dixie nodded. "So now you can remember Little Horse and what he did for you without grieving over it. Won't that be wonderful?"

Danny grew thoughtful. "Someday, I'm going to learn how to handle life like a Christian should, Dixie." He gazed into the fire and whispered, "But it sure seems like I'm a slow learner!"

9

The next weeks were one long disaster as the army tried to pull itself into shape for battle. According to Colonel Washington, even the route General Braddock had chosen to take was a mistake. He sent the army into a wilderness so dense it could not be traveled with heavy cannon.

"We'll have to send woodsmen ahead to cut a road," Washington told Brinkley as Danny worked nearby. "And we'll creep along at such a slow pace, the French will know we're coming days before we even get there."

When Danny relayed this to Dixie, she just shook her head. "Well, we'll just have to go along, even if things don't turn out very well. I don't know any other way of finding Dad." She knit her eyebrows in obvious frustration. "Although so far, no one seems to have heard of him."

One good thing had happened since they had joined the force: Danny had made a friend—Chad Whitesides, a slight fourteen-year-old boy with light blue eyes and blond hair. Chad had never been away from England before—or from home for that matter. Danny had met him while running an errand for Washington. He seemed very young and small to be with an army, and Danny was surprised to learn that many drummer boys were even younger than he was—some as young as twelve.

"I didn't want to come to the army," Chad admitted after they had gotten better acquainted. "But there was nothing to do at home. I had twelve brothers and sisters and I had to go out and make me own way. Only thing I could find to do was join the regiment as a drummer boy."

"Maybe you'll be an officer someday," Danny said. "That'd be good, wouldn't it?"

Chad shook his head. "I don't know. It don't seem likely. Most officers come from rich families, not from poor families like mine."

"You never know what will happen," Danny encouraged him. "Don't give up hope."

As the days passed and the army made no move, Danny grew more anxious. "Chad, do you think this army will ever get started? It seems like we've been stuck here forever."

Chad shook his head. "I don't know. But I wouldn't care if we never did fight." He blushed and looked down at his hands. "I'm not sure what I'd do if the bullets started flying around me. I might turn and run."

Danny felt sorry for him. *If Chad had lived in the twentieth century, he wouldn't be in this mess right now*, he thought. "You won't run. You'll be fine. God will give you courage if you ask Him."

"I don't know much about God," Chad said doubtfully, "but I sure hope you're right."

Danny didn't want to preach, but he didn't want to let the opportunity to tell Chad about God slip by either. "Ever since I became a Christian, Chad, things have been going better for me. Well . . . I guess it's not so much that they always go better—it's more that God gives me the strength to face whatever happens, no matter what it is."

Chad shrugged and looked away. Danny could tell he was embarrassed and decided to wait until later to say more.

Danny had no opportunity to visit with Chad over the next few days. Washington had him running everywhere as he tried to pull the massive army together. Braddock insisted on keeping the force of 1,445 regulars and 262 independent colonial soldiers at an awkward size. Thirty sailors assisted with hauling the cannon and other heavy artillery—the heaviest piece weighed well over half a ton—over the roadless mountains. In addition, there were 449 troops from Virginia, North Carolina, and Maryland, as well as a small detachment of gunners.

Besides artillery, there was a host of necessary supplies—including gunpowder, shot, and shells. A month's supply of food was needed for more than 2,000 men and their horses. It took 150 heavy wagons to carry the supplies. Without the help of Benjamin Franklin, who produced the wagons, the expedition would have been impossible.

"I can't see how we will ever get this train through to the objective!" Washington protested. It was obvious to everyone that he was concerned about the general's plan, even though he had thrown his energies into the attack.

At last the expedition began its slow journey through the forest. "I'm amazed we can even move at all," Danny muttered under his breath as they inched through the dense forest, hacking roads out of the wilderness, crossing swamps, and bridging streams.

It took several days before Braddock realized the advance was taking far too long. He approached Colonel Washington and said, "It's taken five days to move the first fifteen miles. We're going to have to go much faster than this."

Washington shook his head. "Perhaps we ought to leave the train behind and take a fast troop of soldiers ahead. Strike hard," he suggested.

General Braddock puffed visibly. "Absolutely not! We will need to have the guns in order to make the fort surrender."

It was clear to Danny that Braddock only knew one way to fight—by bringing heavy guns up to a fort and using them to force that fort to fall. He had made it known that this tactic had worked for him in England and Europe, and he seemed absolutely certain it would work here in America, too.

That night, after the soldiers had been fed and the animals bedded down, Danny and Dixie met in front of a small fire. Chad came and joined them, looking tired and worn and not at all healthy.

"I wish I were back in England," he said sadly. "Can't no good come of this. I don't know what we English are doing over in this part of the world anyway. This ain't our country."

Danny stared at him. "But, don't you think America belongs to England, Chad?"

The boy shook his head. "It's too far. Way too far. We regulars should have stayed home where we belong."

Danny repeated the conversation to Colonel Washington later that night when he brought him his uniform, clean and ready for the next day.

Washington bit his lip. "I can't say much to that, Danny," he said quietly. "We think of ourselves as Englishmen over here, but Londoners don't seem to understand our problems. They seem to think of this country as nothing but a big farm that they can work and secure supplies from."

"I wonder if they'll ever change their minds," Danny said. He knew the answer, of course, but he wondered whether Washington did, too.

George Washington's face seemed to change. It was as if he saw the future for just one second. "I don't think they will ever change. And if they don't, I think we'll have to change things ourselves."

The long line of wagons and marching troops wound deeper and deeper into the forest, headed for the fork of the Ohio River. The flies and mosquitoes were terrible, and the animals were running out of feed. The Indians and the French they met along the way grew bolder, sometimes stirring up skirmishes, but there was nothing they could do but move forward.

More than once, General Braddock spoke sharply to George Washington in Danny's hearing. Every time, he argued in favor of the battle tactics that had won for the English in Europe.

"We must keep our lines straight and our formations pure. And we must be locked into place," he said during one such conversation. His face was turning red—it seemed to Danny that he always was angry. "I'll have none of your sneaking behind trees and hiding! When we meet up with the French and Indians, one sight of the British line will send them running!"

Washington and others who knew the Indians better tried to convince General Braddock that this approach would not work in America as it had on the flat plains of Europe. But Braddock would not listen.

On and on the force moved. It seemed to Danny and Dixie as if they would never get anywhere. Their boredom turned to excitement when George Washington presented them with some news: "A horse handler told me he knew of a man named Fortune. At least, he thought his name was Fortune. It appears he's one of the woodcutters helping to clear the way for us."

"Oh, sir!" Danny cried, thrilled. "May I go to the front to see?" he asked eagerly.

Washington rubbed his chin. "It's more dangerous up at that part of the line. Several men have been shot by the Indians who lurk in the trees. I'd be afraid for you to go. I will send one of my aides instead."

But Colonel Washington's proposal never took place—he came down with a fever that very night. The next day, he was so weak he could hardly stand. Before sundown, he was forced to crawl into a wagon to ride over the bumpy ground. Danny stayed close to him, making himself available to help whenever Washington's aide wanted something for the sick man.

"He's getting really skinny, Dixie," Danny said when he joined his sister to eat a late supper a couple of days later. "Seems like he can't shake that fever. And the doctor doesn't know what is causing it. You know how doctors in this century are—all he wants to do is bleed him."

"You mean, put a leech on him?"

"Yes. That and purging." Danny grimaced in disgust. "I can't think of anything worse than taking a strong laxative all day long and then getting bled. If a man wasn't sick, he would be by the time the doctors got through with him." He shook his head. "Anyway, he's way too sick for me to bother him about sending someone to the front to learn more about Dad."

"Maybe we should see if Chad can do something. He moves around pretty freely," Dixie suggested, and Danny agreed.

Early the next morning, Danny tracked down Chad. "Say, if you have a chance, could you go up where the men are cutting the trees? Dixie and I are trying to locate a man named James Fortune."

Chad shook his head. "I'd like to, but the sergeant would chop my head off if I left. He wants me at his hand every minute. After all, the men march to my drum. I give the signals, so I have to be right handy." He looked at Danny sadly. "I'd like to go, even though it would be frightening to be up at the head of the line like that. Some of the men have gotten shot up there, you know."

"It was just an idea."

He left and reported this to Dixie. "If nothing else, maybe when the colonel gets better, he'll let me go up. I'll ask him, anyway."

But Colonel Washington grew more and more ill as they went deeper into the forest, ever closer to the guns of Fort Duquesne. Danny had given up any hope of going to the front to search for their father.

"We'll just have to see this expedition through to the end, Dixie. When we get there, we'll find out if Dad is up front with those other men."

10

"I never was so tired of anything!" Danny exclaimed wearily. He threw himself down on the ground beside the log Dixie was sitting on and stared up at her. "How long have we been marching, anyway? It seems like a year!"

Dixie counted the days off on her fingers. "Let's see. This is the fifth—no, the sixth of July. We've been on the road for twenty-four days."

Danny grunted. "It feels like forever. I don't know how much longer we can keep this up. The horses are practically dead. And some of the men aren't much better off."

"Is Colonel Washington any better today?" Dixie asked.

Danny shook his head, then shrugged. "Well, maybe a little. He's lost so much weight, he's nothing but skin and bones. He really needs to be in a hospital."

"There are no hospitals out here, and even the ones in the towns can't be very good," Dixie said. "All we have are these army doctors. They don't seem like they're worth much."

Danny picked up a stick and began to scratch in the ground. "I told Colonel Washington that you and I would be praying for him today. You know what he said? He said, 'Thank you, Danny. And thank Dixie for me. It's God who heals us, and I'm grateful for all the prayers I can get.'"

"Well," Dixie said, "that ought to stop some of Mordecai's nonsense about Washington not being a decent man. He obviously believes in God."

Just as she finished speaking, Chad came ambling over toward them. He was even thinner than he had been at the beginning of the trip, and his clothes, which hadn't been changed for nearly a month, were dirty and torn.

"Hello," he said. "Did you hear what's going to happen?"

Danny looked up at him. "No, what?"

"They're going to detach a part of this force to move forward right away, leaving the rest of the wagons behind."

"Is that right?" Danny asked with interest. "Well, that's what Colonel Washington's been telling General Braddock to do for days. How many are going?"

"The way I heard my sergeant tell it, about 1,400 men with eight cannons and some Howitzers and mortars. Only thirty-four of the wagons will be going."

Dixie rose from her log. "I think I'll go and see if Mrs. Muldoon needs anything. Maybe she'll know more about this."

She left, and Chad sat down beside Danny. He looked a little embarrassed, as if he wanted to say something but wasn't sure where to begin. Finally, he ventured,

"I've been thinking a lot about what you said—especially about God."

Why have you left it up to me to tell him, God? Danny thought nervously, afraid of saying the wrong thing. *Help!* He took a deep breath and began. "Everyone needs to know God, Chad. After all, He made us. He loves us."

Chad looked puzzled. "You think so? How could God love me? I'm no one."

"Don't you remember John 3:16?" Danny asked.

"John three what?" Chad asked with a bewildered look. "What does that mean?"

Danny stared at him in amazement. "John 3:16 is a Bible verse. It says, 'For God so loved the world that he gave his one and only Son, that whoever believes in him shall not perish but have eternal life.' Haven't you ever heard that before?"

Chad shook his head. He looked so sad, slumped over in the falling darkness. Danny wished there were more he could do. "I don't think anyone ever loved me," he admitted in a low tone. "My mother and father didn't have time for it. They were always working—all of us were always working. I guess I don't know much about love." He stared at the ground, then lifted his eyes to Danny's. "You say it says in the Bible that God loves us. Does that mean all of us, or just some of us?"

"Why, all of us!" Danny said. "God doesn't pick favorites. He loves you just as much as he loves anyone else, Chad."

Chad sat quietly. After a while, he said, "Well, that's good news." He grew silent again, and Danny said nothing to interrupt his friend's thoughts.

A few more minutes of silence passed, then Chad asked, "What do you think happens to us when we die?"

"If we know Jesus, we go straight to heaven."

The answer caught Chad's attention, and he said immediately, "I'd like that! I don't know much about heaven, but it's got to be better than anything I've known here. Tell me about it, will you?"

Danny was suddenly thankful for all the years of Sunday school and memorizing scriptures about heaven. To his surprise, the right words seemed to flow out of him.

Taking a deep breath, he concluded, "You know, Chad, I think it would be a good idea if you asked God to make you ready for heaven right now." He flinched a little, afraid Chad would be offended. But when he looked at him through the falling gloom, he thought he saw the glint of tears in his eyes.

"How do I do that?" Chad asked.

"I'll pray for you—if you want," Danny began, then felt surprised at his own bold suggestion. "You can pray along with me and ask God to forgive you for any wrong you have done. Tell Him you are sorry and that you want to be saved through His Son, Jesus."

"I guess I can do that," Chad said, bowing his head.

Danny prayed a quick prayer.

When he had finished, Chad looked up at him and asked, "Is that all I need to do?"

Danny nodded. "That's all any of us can do. Jesus already paid the price for our salvation. All we can do is accept what He offers us."

They sat on the log for a while longer. At last Chad

stood. "I feel so much better now, Danny. It's as though a load has been lifted off my shoulders."

"Remember that Dixie and I'll be praying for you and your safety in the middle of battle. But if something does happen, keep in mind that Jesus will always be with you—whether here or in heaven."

"I'll remember," Chad whispered, walking off into the darkness.

Danny headed back to the campfire, praying that God would take care of his friend in the battle he knew was to come.

Danny and Dixie learned the disappointing news that Dixie was to be left behind as the smaller force made its way forward.

"I'm afraid of being separated, Danny," she confided before he left. "Especially here. What if something happens?"

Danny knew immediately what she meant. "I've been thinking about that," he said, reaching into his shirt. "I want you to keep the Recall Unit—you know, just in case. That way, at least you'll be able to return home if . . . if things get bad."

Dixie took the device and hung it around her neck. "Be careful, Danny," she said, her eyes dark with concern. "I'd hate for something to happen to you." She gave him a quick hug and forced a smile.

"I'll be okay, Dix. Just pray for me—and pray that I'll find Dad, too," he added around the suspicious lump that had formed in his throat.

The detachment, including a very weak Colonel George Washington, proceeded into the wilderness. On July 7, they camped close to the Monongahela River. Danny took some soup to the colonel and sat with him as he tried to eat it. He set down the soup after eating only half.

"You really need to eat all you can, Colonel Washington," Danny said. "You need to keep up your strength."

Washington smiled wanly, his face drawn and thin. "I know you're right, but I just don't have any appetite." He picked the bowl back up, took another few spoonfuls, then handed the rest to Danny. "That's all I can eat. Thank you."

Danny took the bowl and turned to leave, then stopped and looked at Washington. "Can I get you anything else before you go to bed?"

"No, I think I'll turn in now," the man responded wearily.

Danny knew he should wait for a better time, but he couldn't resist asking, "I hear that we're very close to Fort Duquesne now. Do you think there'll be a battle soon?"

Colonel Washington got to his feet. The fever had made him lose so much weight that he looked more like a skeleton than a man. He took a deep breath, then leaned heavily against the wagon where his bed was made. "I'm surprised we haven't been attacked before this," he said tiredly. "They know we're coming. Their scouts have been all around us for days. They're fools if they don't attack us before we reach the fort."

Danny thought about that. "Do you think we can win?"

Washington looked down at his thin hands, then lifted his gaze to Danny's. "That's in the hands of God, I'm sure. We've done all that men can do. Now all we can do is pray that the Almighty will be with us and keep us."

"I'll pray for that, too, sir," Danny said. He went back to his own pallet, which was near a campfire. Chad was there, too.

"You know, Danny," he said, "I'm not afraid of fighting anymore."

"You're not?"

"Everything's been so different ever since you and I prayed and I asked Jesus to come into my heart," Chad admitted. "Before, I was afraid of almost everything. But since that night, everything's been . . . calm, I guess you could say." He leaned on one elbow and stared up at the sky. "I don't know how to describe it. I feel as though, before, I was living in the middle of a huge storm. The waves were high and the lightning was flashing. I was struggling just to float. And now, it's as if I'm floating on a calm, glassy sea. Everything's better, even though now I'm in more danger than ever before."

He stared across the fire at Danny. "Do you feel like that, too?"

Danny nodded. "Sometimes. And if I don't, it's because I've forgotten God is with me." He yawned and pulled his blanket snugly up to his chin to keep the bugs away. "We'd better go to sleep. It's going to be a long day tomorrow."

He rolled over and thought for a long time about the coming battle. He had not been completely honest with Chad. Even though he knew he was saved, the idea of being shot or wounded or captured by the Indians still sent a tingle of fear through him.

Why do I have such a hard time trusting God to take care of me? he wondered. His heart beating quickly, he whispered a prayer for safety—this time for all of them.

11

By dawn, the army was headed through the dense forest. They were now on the south bank of Turtle Creek, which flowed into the shallow waters of the Mononga-hela. Braddock had decided to cross it, march past the mouth of Turtle Creek, then cross back to the same side of the river as Fort Duquesne.

Danny stayed close to Colonel Washington, walking alongside the wagon that carried him.

"Danny," came Washington's weak voice, "have one of my aides saddle my horse and bring it up."

Danny stared at him, not sure he had heard correctly. After twenty days of illness, Washington didn't look capable of even sitting up, let alone riding a horse.

"You're not strong enough to ride, sir," Danny said carefully.

Washington shook his head stubbornly. "I know what I'm doing. Get the horse!"

Danny rushed to inform Brinkley of the colonel's decision. He watched as the aide saddled Washington's big horse.

By the time they returned, Washington was up and ready to go. He moved slowly to the horse and stared at the saddle. "Danny, I'm nothing but bones. Get that pillow out of the wagon for me, please."

"Yes, sir." Danny grabbed one of the feather pillows out of the wagon and placed it in the saddle. Colonel Washington carefully pulled himself into the padded seat.

He swayed dangerously, and Brinkley said, "Sir, you're not fit for this."

Washington only shook his head and touched the horse with his heels.

As he left, Brinkley looked at Danny, doubt on his face. "I wish he wouldn't ride, but you never could tell that man anything." He turned and mounted his own horse; soon, he was riding beside Washington.

Danny plodded along, always keeping the colonel and his aide in sight as the red-coated regulars splashed into the stream to make the second crossing. When his turn arrived, the cool water was welcome. The July heat was unbearable—he was sure it was even worse for the soldiers, whose uniforms were designed for cool English weather.

The river was so low that it exposed a pebbled beach. Braddock took full advantage of the space to parade his army, drums beating and trumpets blaring.

The driver of Washington's wagon grinned at Danny. "Guess that's supposed to scare the Indians away," he laughed.

Danny moved faster, trying to keep pace with Washington and his aide.

"I suppose General Braddock thinks this parading will impress the enemy," he overheard Washington say.

"But I doubt it will have much effect on their marksmanship."

"I'd rather we sent out more scouts," Brinkley said. "Have you talked to General Braddock about the attack?"

"Are you referring to letting the men take cover?" Washington asked. He shook his head. "I tried, but he only said, 'There'll be no hiding behind trees.' "

"You'll pardon my saying it, but he's a fool, sir," Brinkley observed. "Look at those troops! Why, it'd be impossible for a marksman to miss them!"

Danny had to admit that the brilliant scarlet coats and the high red mitre caps stood out like flames against the green woods.

Brinkley shook his head. "If they jump us, we're finished."

Washington didn't answer, but when General Braddock led the line of troops into a thicket lined on both sides with towering trees and thick ground cover, he said, "I don't like this ground."

He had no sooner spoken than a volley of shots rang out. Three red-coated troopers fell to the ground. "It's a trap!" he shouted, spurring his horse.

He drove past the line of soldiers to pull up beside Braddock. "Sir!" he said, "there's a walnut grove back there. We can pull back and see the enemy."

Braddock stared at him as if he were insane. "Retreat? From this rabble? Absolutely not. You may now see how the British soldier handles an enemy." Galloping ahead, his face red with rage, he ordered Colonel Burton to bring his troops forward. He galloped up, sword drawn, and began beating his own men away from the trees, crying, "Charge!"

The troops moved forward, but the firing from the bushes became more intense.

"Sir!" Washington shouted. "This is the main force!"

"Nonsense! It's just a few skirmishers," Braddock scoffed. He gave a command, and the English fired into the forest. Their musket balls cut leaves from the trees and splintered saplings, but the enemy remained firmly entrenched behind the huge trees. They clearly knew that the British, now that they had fired, would have to reload. The enemy came zigzagging through the trees like phantoms, always firing. More Redcoats dropped to the ground.

Suddenly, the general's horse reared as a musket ball struck its flanks, dumping Braddock onto the ground. He mounted another horse and shouted, "Forward! Charge the enemy!"

A wall of red filled the road as the massive force of men walked shoulder to shoulder into the gunfire. Behind them were the entire flying column, the militia, and the Virginia blues.

The woods blazed with musket shots, and bullets hailed from the unsecured sights. Within minutes, the outer columns were shot to bits, and the cries of dying men were everywhere. In an effort to maintain control, the officers ordered their men to face the right and march in formation—right into the deadly woods. There was no target in sight.

Why, we're walking into a trap! Danny thought. To fight under these conditions seemed like suicide.

But Colonel George Washington surprised Danny by suddenly coming alive in the saddle. As General Braddock's aides were killed and wounded, one by one, he worked feverishly to carry out the general's orders. Danny didn't know how he found the strength. He seemed to be everywhere at once. His tall figure and saddle perch should have made him an easy mark for the screaming bullets, but nothing could knock him from his horse. Danny was amazed as he watched the bullets whiz by Washington, four leaving burns where they cut through his coat. Two horses were shot out from under him, but each time he cleared the tumbling animal and quickly mounted another.

All Danny could do was try to keep out of the way among the wagoneers, who were fighting from their wagons. Bullets whistled and thumped into the walls of his wagon as the Indians and the French came at them from both sides. He looked wildly around for a place to hide, but there was nowhere to run. He was sure the enemy had closed off every line of retreat. *Better stay where I am and pray*, he thought desperately.

After three hours of intense fighting, Braddock finally gave up hope. The white sash he wore made him an easy target, and he had been under fire all afternoon. Four horses had fallen dead beneath him. With his army demoralized, he sent Washington to advise the captains to retreat.

Washington had hardly left his side before General Braddock cried out. He had been hit! A bullet had passed through his arm and into his chest, and he fell to the ground. Some soldiers picked him up and carried him in a litter to one of the abandoned wagons.

Since the general was wounded, Colonel Washington took command, organizing the retreat, sending for help from the troops they'd left behind, and taking care of the wounded. He somehow managed to be everywhere at once. *We'd all die if it weren't for him*, Danny thought.

When the colonel had a chance to speak to Danny again, he met him with a serious expression. "I've learned something here today," he said seriously. "European tactics will never win a victory in this country."

Danny had to agree. *And just wait till twenty years from now, Colonel Washington, when you get to prove it again. But next time, it will be we Americans fighting against the English!*

When they finally had time to make a count of the troops, they were horrified to learn of the result: Of the 1,451 who had crossed the river at noon, 456 were dead, 421 wounded, and a dozen taken prisoner. Danny had never imagined such devastation.

As the bedraggled force of men came out of the forest followed by rows of staggering soldiers and wagons full of wounded, he wondered how they appeared to those they'd left behind. *I hope Dixie's okay*, Danny thought as he walked alongside one of the last wagons.

"Danny! Danny!" His sister burst out of the anxious crowd that had gathered to meet them. She threw her arms around him and squeezed. "You're all right!"

Danny was so tired he could hardly walk, and he'd

never felt more filthy and depressed in his life. He leaned on Dixie for a second to catch his breath, then stepped back. "Yes, I'm okay," he said.

"What about Chad?" Dixie asked. "Is he all right, too?"

Danny hesitated, then shook his head. "I'm afraid not. He was badly wounded. He's . . . he's in this wagon."

His sister began to hurry toward the wagon, and Danny put a hand on her shoulder to stop her. In a low voice, he said, "Dixie, I don't think he's going to make it."

Tears came to her eyes, and she nodded slowly. "Then he needs us more than ever," she said, following the wagon until it rolled to a stop.

Dixie pulled a blanket from the wagon and laid it on the ground, then helped Danny take Chad out of the wagon and place him on it. She held his hand as they waited for the surgeon.

"He took a bullet in the stomach," Danny said. "They say no one can live after that."

When at last the surgeon came by, he pulled the blanket back, took one look at the bloody front of Chad's shirt, and shook his head. "Nothing I can do for him," he said brusquely before moving on.

The twins sat beside the wounded boy for hours. Dixie washed his face with cool water, but he didn't respond. His breathing was shallow, and he never opened his eyes.

Finally, after Dixie had fallen into an exhausted sleep beside him, Chad's eyelids trembled, and he opened his eyes.

"Chad," Danny whispered, "can you hear me?"

He licked his lips, and Danny moistened them with a rag soaked in cool water. "Don't try to move," he said. "Just stay still."

Chad looked at him, then raised his head to look down at the bloodied front of his shirt. "I'm going to die, aren't I, Danny?" he whispered.

"Don't say that!" Danny said.

Chad shook his head slowly, wincing at the movement. He spoke again in a hoarse whisper. "Don't take on so," he said. "Don't you remember what you told me that time we prayed?"

Danny took Chad's hand and held it so tightly his own hand hurt. "I remember, Chad," he said.

They remained silent for a while, then, "I've thought about it since I was shot. Everybody who trusts in Jesus, if they die, they go to be with Him. Ain't that right?"

"That's exactly right," Danny said.

Chad smiled faintly. "Well, then, I'm all right." He didn't say anything else for so long that Danny began to think he had died.

Then, without warning, he opened his eyes wide and said with surprise, "Why, it *is* all right. Dying's not bad. It's not what I thought it was. . . ." His voice trailed off, and Danny bent closer to catch the last words as they came. "It's not bad, Danny. . ." he whispered. "It's . . . just . . . going . . . to be with . . . Jesus."

Tears ran down Danny's face, falling on the now lifeless body below. "Thank you, Lord," he whispered. "Thank you that I got to tell Chad about Jesus."

12

Danny couldn't sleep that night. The disheveled mob that had fled from the field wandered around the camp, never straying far from the wagon in which Braddock was lying.

Despite the wounds to his arm and lung, the general was conscious—enough so to compliment Washington for organizing the rear guard. He ordered that the camp be put in a defensive position so that the enemy could not attack.

Washington, weak almost to the point of dropping off his horse, rode into the moonlit hours in his search for wounded. He could barely see as he and a small guard rode back through the stumps to the scene of the battle. At times, he told Danny later that night, their horses stepped on soldiers, wounded and dying, lying in the dirt where they'd fallen from exhaustion.

After surveying the terrain, Washington and his aides returned to the camp and General Braddock. "Sir," he said, "I do not think we need fear attack. The Indians and the French seem to have given up and gone back to Fort Duquesne."

Braddock nodded feebly. He could barely speak, and his face was as pale as the moon above. "Take the army back, Colonel."

For three days, the army struggled back over the same road they had used to get to Fort Duquesne. But by the fourth day, it was clear to everyone that General Braddock was near death. They stopped. That night, the general remarked to an officer, "Who would have thought it?" Immediately afterward, he lapsed into unconsciousness and died.

The next morning, Washington chose a burial place in the middle of the road at the head of the column. The chaplain was too severely wounded to officiate at the funeral, and the other officers did not seem to know how. But Colonel Washington had buried men before—at Fort Necessity. He drew a prayer book from his baggage and began to read the Anglican service.

"I am the Resurrection and the Life." He paused, and Danny and Dixie were close enough to see the sorrow on his face as he spoke a few kind words about the dead man.

When at last the shrouded body had been lowered into the grave, Washington ordered that every wagon tire, every horse's hoof, and every man's foot should march over the grave, pounding the mound down. Nothing was left to mark its place, or a passing Indian would dig up the grave for its graying scalp and general's uniform.

Dixie and Danny trudged along as best they could. All the wagons had been burned, except for a few carrying supplies, to keep the enemy from getting them.

"I still can't believe Chad is gone. First Little Horse, now Chad. At least this time I had a chance to be a true friend."

"Yes," Dixie replied. "When we first met him, Chad was so afraid—of everything. And he had had such a tough life."

Danny nodded. "You know, he told me once that no one had ever loved him. Not even his parents." He went on to tell his sister more about his talks with Chad. "I don't know, but it seems to me like God just made it so I could talk to Chad. Do you think He does things like that? God, I mean?"

Dixie nodded. "Sure. Just think—He used you to help Chad come to Jesus before it was too late."

The gloom that had settled on Danny lifted, and he thought about his friends Little Horse and Chad, knowing he would see them both again someday in heaven.

The next day, one of the men who had served as a scout for the expedition approached the twins as they marched along. He was a tall man, who wore a fringed leather shirt and carried his long rifle cradled in his arms almost like a child. "The colonel, he tells me you was looking for a man called James."

Danny felt a sudden burst of excitement. "Yes! Do you know him?"

The scout looked carefully at Danny and Dixie. "Is he a relative of yourn?"

"We . . . we think so," Dixie said breathlessly.

The scout took several paces, then shook his head. "Well, I *did* know him, but I fear I've got bad news for you."

"Wh-what is it?" Danny stammered, although he could already read the answer in the scout's face. "Was he killed in the battle?"

"I'm afeared that's the way of it," the man responded. He studied the twins. "I got to know him pretty good. As a matter of fact, I knowed him before the battle. Run into him in the hills back in the Shenandoah valley. And when I come to be with the militia, James, he come, too."

Danny blinked. Had so much time already passed for his father? "Are you sure his name was Fortune?" he asked. "F-O-R-T-U-N-E?"

The scout looked confused, then shook his head. "Why, no—not that. It was Fordun! F-O-R-D-U-N."

"Are you certain?" Dixie asked quickly.

"Plumb sure. Like I said, I met his family in the Shenandoah. Why, the Forduns been there, seems like forever."

"Thank you for coming to talk to us," Danny said, his heart beating normally again. "But I don't think he's the man we're looking for."

"Just thought I'd let you know—in case."

As he wandered off, Dixie turned to her brother. "Well, I never thought I would be so glad to hear we were following up on a false lead."

"Me either." Danny shook his head. "What do we do now?"

"I think we need to go home. It looks to me as if this

isn't the right time or place for Dad. Maybe we can wander off as soon as we get back to camp. There's so much confusion, no one will miss us."

"All right," Danny conceded, "but I think we should talk with George Washington before we leave. He thinks we're coming back with him to Mount Vernon."

⚡ ⚡ ⚡

Danny and Dixie had to wait until they approached Cumberland, where the army was to be stationed, to speak privately with the busy Washington. They found him inside the fort store buying supplies.

"Please, Colonel Washington, sir, could we talk with you for a minute?"

He turned and smiled. "Of course. I'm almost through here." He paid for his purchases, nodded at the clerk, then walked out ahead of the twins.

When they were outside, he looked at them and said soberly, "I heard about the man we were inquiring after. I understand he was no relation to you after all."

"No, his name was Fordun, not Fortune," Danny said.

"We'll just have to continue to look, then," Colonel Washington said, his eyebrows knit into a serious expression.

"Sir," Dixie asked, "in the long run, will it hurt us that we lost the battle?"

Washington glanced at her, then shook his head. "No, not really. Terrible as it was, we've learned something from this. We'll not try to fight Indians in English formation anymore."

The sun was bright as they walked along, and Washington seemed to be in a cheerful mood. "This war has been going on a long time, but I believe we will win in the end. We're going to cross over those mountains yet."

Danny was amazed at Washington's vision for the future—even at such a relatively young age, he seemed like a man capable of leading a new nation.

"I suppose you'll be going back to Mount Vernon?" he finally asked.

"Uh . . . no, sir," Danny answered. "Dixie and I have decided to search somewhere else—maybe Philadelphia."

Dixie gave Danny a quick look as if to say, *Oh, really?*

"I suppose you have friends there," Washington said. "If it might be of service, I can write to some friends of mine there. They might help you find work."

"That would be kind of you, sir."

"Then, come along. I'll write that letter right now." The colonel made his way through the fort to the small office he had been using since the army's return. He sat down and took out a piece of paper, grabbing a turkey quill from a holder. He dabbed the quill in a bottle of ink and started to write.

"Oh dear," he said. "This bottle's out of ink. Let me see if I can find some more." He rummaged through the desk, but there was none to be found.

Without thinking, Danny said, "I have a pen, Colonel Washington."

He reached into his inner pocket and pulled out a

ball-point pen he had brought by mistake.

"Danny, I don't think—" Dixie began.

But it was too late. Colonel Washington already had the pen and was examining it. "I hardly see how this would work, Danny," he said. "We still don't have any ink. And it doesn't look as if it would hold it well, anyway."

Danny was trapped. He stammered, "Well . . . this is a new type of pen, sir. It carries the ink inside."

"Ink inside a pen?" Washington asked in surprise. He held it up and said suddenly, "Why, I can almost see through this thing. Is it made out of glass?"

"Not exactly," Danny said, heartily wishing he had never given Washington the pen. He took it back. "You hold it like this, sir, to write. And the ink flows down through the tip. See? Try it."

Washington gingerly put the tip of the ball-point on the paper, made a slight movement, then exclaimed, "Well, look at that!" His face was alive with interest as he slowly wrote a word, watching with fascination as the pen traced the letters across the paper. "I never saw anything like this. Where was this pen made?"

Danny gave Dixie an agonized glance. "I . . . I . . . uh think somewhere in . . . Asia. China, maybe." He had no idea where the pen was made, but he knew most things like it were made in Taiwan and other Asian countries. All he could think was, *Mordecai will kill me! He's told me never to take anything from the present into the past and vice versa. Now what am I going to do?*

"Look!" Colonel Washington noted as he finished the letter. "You don't even have to sprinkle any sand on the ink to dry it! I've never seen anything like this!"

It was obvious he would have loved to keep the pen, but Danny knew he couldn't give it to him. "This was a gift," he said, putting his hand out for the ball-point.

Washington handed the pen back reluctantly. "I would be most gratified if you let me know if you found another. There's a fortune to be made in a thing like this." He made a face. "You know how much trouble it is, trimming these confounded turkey feathers. And keeping ink and sand and all of that. Why, this would revolutionize the art of writing."

He stood and handed Danny the letter. "I hope this helps you."

Danny took the letter, folded it carefully, and slipped it into his pocket.

"Before we leave, I want to thank you, Colonel, for all you've done for us. And would you please say good-bye to everyone back at Mount Vernon?"

"I'll do that, my boy." Washington put out his hand, and Danny shook it. Then he shook hands with Dixie. "You know, it's only by the grace of Providence that I've been protected from death in battle. I pray that the same Almighty power that kept me in battle will keep you two as you go on your way."

Danny was overwhelmed by Washington's words.

"Goodbye, Colonel," they said as they walked away.

"C'mon, let's get out of here," Dixie said once they were out of hearing. "I want to get home and tell Mordecai about this."

They made their way deep into the woods outside the

fort. "Have you still got the Recall Unit?" Danny asked her.

She waved it in her hand, her thumb poised over the button. "Are you ready?"

"I'm ready," said Danny.

They took one last look around, and Dixie said, "I wish Colonel Washington could know what wonderful things are going to happen to him."

"So do I," Danny said, then added, "Oh, wait—just one more thing." He took the letter from his pocket and stared at it. "This would be worth a fortune if we took it back," he said.

"We can't do that, Danny," Dixie said. "Mordecai says we can't take *anything* back from the past, no matter how great it is."

Danny sighed and tore the paper up into tiny pieces. "Goodbye, fortune!"

Then Dixie pushed the button.

13

Danny had ridden a wild roller coaster once at a theme park. Returning from the past felt like that moment at the bottom of a plunge when the car hit the lower curve and twisted sideways—he felt like he was being wrenched in two directions at once!

Slowly, the sensation left and the vibration ceased. The pale green fog faded away, and the figures of Mordecai and Zacharias Fortune solidified before his eyes.

Danny gave his sister a quick glance. "You okay, Dix?" He knew she was prone to motion sickness—and the Chrono-Shuttle was anything but gentle with the people it transported.

She took a deep breath and nodded. "Yes. I'm all right—only let's get out of this crazy thing!"

Mordecai was already opening the Plexiglas door so they could clamber out of the Chrono-Shuttle. "Well?" he asked eagerly. "Did you see him? Did you see George Washington?" His eyes were gleaming with anticipation.

"Let us get our feet on the ground before you start with the questions, okay?" Danny protested. Even though the twins had time traveled before, coming back and readjusting still seemed strange. Danny *knew* they had been gone for weeks, yet when he glanced at the clock and calendar on the wall, he saw that the date was the same as when they had left. In fact, they had been gone no more than an hour!

"I can never get used to the way this works," he said. "Here, Dixie, why don't you sit down a minute?"

"I'm all right," she returned weakly. But she sat down anyway.

"Let me get you two something to drink, and then we'll talk about your trip. It's obvious you didn't find your father—and terribly unfortunate—but how was the trip? Would you like some hot cocoa?"

"Oh, that would be nice," Dixie said. "Thanks."

"Let's go into my study, then," Mordecai said, "and we'll have a nice chat with you two while you have a little something to eat."

They left the laboratory and climbed the stairs to Mordecai's dusty study, while Zacharias scurried to fix them hot cocoa. He served it on a silver tray with some Oreos and Twinkies.

"I'm afraid this is all we have," he said, shaking his head sadly. "We're not exactly health food fans in this house."

Danny took an Oreo and bit into it. "Boy, have I missed modern food!"

As the twins got started on their snack, Mordecai jumped right in. "All right, let's get down to business. I want to hear everything."

For the next hour, Danny and Dixie talked steadily—that is, when Mordecai wasn't interrupting for more details. He recorded their conversation so he could go over their report again later.

Finally, the historian shook his head. "This doesn't help me very much. It throws some light on Braddock's crusade against Fort Duquesne, but it doesn't tell me a whole lot about George Washington."

"Well, I can tell you a *lot* about Washington!" Danny said eagerly. "He was one of the best men—and leaders—I've ever known. He certainly didn't remind me of the power-hungry politicians you see so much of today. He actually cared about other people, and he credited God with protecting him from danger."

Mordecai pulled at his beard. "Yes, well, that could just be politician talk. You'll notice that when politicians are running for office or get into trouble, they drag God into it. They never mean anything by it. No, I'm still not satisfied. He couldn't have been the man *other* historians have made him out to be."

He got up and paced the room, still tugging at his beard. Then he turned and said, "It was the wrong time. He was too young. After all, he was only twenty-three when he accompanied Braddock. No man's got any sense when he's only twenty-three!"

Dixie stared at him. "That's the craziest thing I ever heard. Age doesn't mean anything."

Mordecai glared at her. "Well, that's what you think!" he snapped. "But I say that the real Washington didn't appear until later, when he was more mature. After he became famous and acquired fans—ah yes, that's when you find out what a man really is!"

Zacharias added, "You know, I think Mordecai has

something there. Youth doesn't necessarily test a man. Sometimes age tests him. We'd have to see more of Washington to know what kind of a person he really was in the end."

Danny suddenly realized what they were getting at. "I suppose this means you're asking Dixie and me to go back and visit George Washington later in time—maybe during the Revolution?"

Mordecai shrugged his shoulders and gave them his most innocent look. "Why, you are always so suspicious, Danny! But, after all, the importance of going is obvious, isn't it?"

"What's obvious?" Dixie asked.

"Why, if your father wasn't with Washington during the French and Indian War, chances are that he chose to go during the most prominent time of Washington's life. I suppose I should have thought of that in the first place."

Zacharias nodded soberly. "I'm afraid Mordecai's right. Your father did talk a lot about the Revolution. It was the heart of his studies as a historian. I wouldn't be a bit surprised if he didn't choose to visit that time." He shrugged his thin shoulders, adding, "Too bad you had to waste the time, but"—he brightened as he glanced at the clock—"the last trip only took an hour. Surely you can spend an hour of your life looking for your father?"

Dixie wrinkled her forehead. "Wait a minute," she said. "You two have only aged an hour. But what about us? We've been gone for—I don't know, months, it seems like. Maybe we've actually aged that much. How would we know?"

Danny's eyes popped open. "Wait a minute. If that's true and we keep spending months and even years in the past, we'll be old before we're fifteen!" He groaned and shut his eyes. "It makes my head ache just to think about it!"

"Oh, I don't think you need to worry about that," Mordecai said smoothly. "You don't look any older to me than you did when you left. And, anyway," he added slyly, "you do trust God to take care of you, don't you?"

Danny glared at him. He knew neither of his great-uncles had any faith in God. The pair never lost a chance to belittle other people's dependence on Him. But Danny remained quiet; Mordecai was too fond of arguing.

"Either way, I don't want to talk about it any more right now. We need to get home and give the money to Mom so she can enroll Jimmy in the new treatment program as soon as possible."

"Have it your way," Mordecai said, raising his hands. "But I imagine you'll need to take a moment to change clothes first." He smiled brightly. "You can't go back home wearing those things, can you now?"

Danny and Dixie changed back into their everyday clothes. Danny hadn't mentioned the incident with the ball-point pen or the letter to their oddball relatives. *Some things are better left unsaid*, he thought. *Especially where our great-uncles are concerned.*

When they were ready, he checked his pocket to make sure the thick envelope of money was still there.

It was. "Thanks for the help," he said. "Jimmy isn't here to thank you, so thanks for him, too."

"Don't mention it," Mordecai said generously. He laid his hand carefully on Danny's shoulder and whispered, "And I'm sure we'll be seeing you two again quite soon. I can't imagine that you'd let your poor, poor father linger in the past. What kind of a son would you be if you did?"

Danny stared at him. "I can't believe you. Of course, we'll be back! Dixie and I can't let Dad stay in the past. I'll give you a call tomorrow to let you know what's happening. We might even be out tomorrow night.

"In the meantime," he went on, "I'd be thinking about the best spot for us to visit during Revolutionary times. We can't afford to keep making mistakes."

"Of course. Don't worry about it. We'll put our whole attention to it." Mordecai beamed. "Won't we, Zacharias?"

"Yes, of course," his twin agreed. "And do give our best regards to your dear mother and brother," he added.

The twins called for a taxi and the same nervous cab driver came to pick them up. As they climbed in, he said, "I'm surprised you two lasted out here as long as you did. I wouldn't have anything to do with them two creeps in there."

"How do you know they're creepy?" Dixie asked curiously. "Have you met them?"

The driver shrugged. "Nah. But everyone round here knows they're crazy. Some kind of mad scientists or something."

Dixie and Danny said nothing for the rest of the ride. They knew that anything they had to say would only confirm the cabbie's suspicions about their great-uncles, and they didn't want to jeopardize their plan to find their father.

He let them out in front of their apartment building, and Danny paid the fare. He watched as the cab drove out of sight, then said, "Well, we didn't find Dad." He shook his head sadly. "Sometimes I wonder if we ever will."

Dixie patted him on the back. "We will. Don't worry. In the meantime, just think about how much good this money's going to do Jimmy. C'mon, let's go tell him about it!"

The next morning, Ellen Fortune took Jimmy to the hospital and made arrangements for him to begin his new treatment.

As they headed to school that day, Dixie said, "Can you believe all that's happened since yesterday?"

"No. It seems impossible!" Danny laughed. "And now I'll be even more likely than ever to say something I shouldn't in history class!"

Things went surprisingly well for Danny. That is, until he again found himself in history class. As he entered the classroom, Courtney Johnson passed by, giving him a smile that nearly melted the enamel on his teeth. She leaned over so close he could smell her perfume. "Don't let Mrs. Simpkins run all over you, Danny," she whispered.

It would have been better if she had not said anything. Suddenly, Danny lost his determination to keep his mouth shut in history class. As soon as Mrs. Simpkins began to talk about the *Mayflower*, getting her facts wrong as usual, Danny opened his mouth.

"I'm afraid that's not quite right, Mrs. Simpkins."

His teacher gave him a stony-eyed glare. "Would you like to come up and teach the class, Danny?"

"Oh no," he replied quickly, his face turning red. "I'm just really interested in history."

Mrs. Simpkins nodded briefly. "That's fine. But in order to learn it well, you need to go on to college—maybe even on to graduate school. Why, I've been going to school now for years, and I still haven't begun to learn all there is to know about the subject."

Danny wanted to say, "You got that right," but he had sense enough to keep his mouth shut this time.

He tuned out as Mrs. Simpkins resumed her lecture. *Maybe I should ask Courtney to have a Coke with me after the game on Saturday*, he thought. *At least she doesn't have any beefy young pioneers like William hanging around her!*

Lost in his thoughts, Danny didn't notice when the bell rang. He was too late to catch Courtney now. He spotted her in the crowd of students leaving the room. She was talking to Matt Taylor.

Great, Danny thought. *Even though Matt doesn't have a lot upstairs, a jock like him has a better chance of getting Courtney's attention than a guy like me.*

"Why didn't you ask her out, Danny?"

Surprised, Danny whirled to find Dixie standing behind him.

"You read my mind," he said. "I don't know if I like the idea of having a mind-reading twin sister right now."

"Don't worry about it. I won't tell." She grinned, revealing her crooked teeth—teeth that a week ago she would have been too shy to show. "Anyway, you don't have to be a twin to know you're interested in Courtney. It's written all over your face. And I don't see why. She hasn't got a brain in her head."

"I know," Danny sighed. "But she sure is pretty. And just wait—someday she's going to pay attention to me. I'm going to do something great that'll make her notice me."

"Say, I have something I want to show you. I found an interesting paragraph in the library today," Dixie said, changing the subject. "I've got it right here. It's about General Braddock."

"What about him?" Danny asked.

"Well, you remember how the colonel had us all march over his burial spot so the Indians wouldn't be able to find it? Listen to what I discovered in this book." She began to read:

" 'The general slept in that forgotten place until 1824. Then, when workmen were grading for a new road, they excavated human bones. With them, they found the medal insignia of a British general and knew they had accidentally dug up Braddock's grave. They reburied the bones nearby, and today a monument marks the location. Thousands of travelers on U.S. Highway 40 pause there, remembering him not for the glory he had won in Europe, but for his inglorious defeat at the Battle of Monongahela. Yet despite his blunders, he was a brave man.' "

Dixie closed the history book. "I'm glad they found him. He didn't do very well as a general here, but he did the best he knew how."

Danny agreed. "You're right, Dixie. He did do the best he knew how—and that's all any of us can do."

Suddenly, a thought came to Danny. "You know, I really can't wait to see what George Washington was like in the year 1776. Do you think he'll recognize us?"

"I don't know," Dixie said thoughtfully. "I hope not. Maybe we could disguise ourselves in some way."

"I hadn't thought of that," Danny admitted. "I've just been thinking how amazing it would be to meet Benjamin Franklin and Thomas Jefferson and all the other heroes of the Revolution."

As they stepped onto the bus, Dixie said excitedly, "Let's leave tonight, Danny. We can look for Dad, and we can see the Revolution!"

Teen Series From
Bethany House Publishers

~~~~

Early Teen Fiction (11–14)

HIGH HURDLES by Lauraine Snelling
Show jumper DJ Randall strives to defy the odds and achieve her dream of winning Olympic Gold.

SUMMERHILL SECRETS by Beverly Lewis
Fun-loving Merry Hanson encounters mystery and excitement in Pennsylvania's Amish country.

THE TIME NAVIGATORS by Gilbert Morris
Travel back in time with Danny and Dixie as they explore unforgettable moments in history.

Young Adult Fiction (12 and up)

CEDAR RIVER DAYDREAMS by Judy Baer
Experience the challenges and excitement of high school life with Lexi Leighton and her friends—over one million books sold!

GOLDEN FILLY SERIES by Lauraine Snelling
Readers are in for an exhilarating ride as Tricia Evanston races to become the first female jockey to win the sought-after Triple Crown.

JENNIE MCGRADY MYSTERIES by Patricia Rushford
A contemporary Nancy Drew, Jennie McGrady's sleuthing talents promise to keep readers on the edge of their seats.

LIVE! FROM BRENTWOOD HIGH by Judy Baer
When eight teenagers invade the newsroom, the result is an action-packed teen-run news show exploring the love, laughter, and tears of high school life.

THE SPECTRUM CHRONICLES by Thomas Locke
Adventure and romance await readers in this fantasy series set in another place and time.

SPRINGSONG BOOKS by various authors
Compelling love stories and contemporary themes promise to capture the hearts of readers.

WHITE DOVE ROMANCES by Yvonne Lehman
Romance, suspense, and fast-paced action for teens committed to finding pure love.

9605

HOLDEMAN CHURCH PROPERTY